David Bell has been writing stories since he was a child.

Now, as a fully grown-up child, he still writes every day.

Dawn Gray is his first comic trilogy.

dawn gray's cosmic adventure

David Bell

Ransom

Dawn Gray's Cosmic Adventure

by David Bell
Cover illustration by Duncan Gutteridge

Published by Ransom Publishing Ltd.
Rose Cottage, Howe Hill, Watlington, Oxon. OX49 5HB
www.ransom.co.uk

ISBN   184167 558 X
         978 184167 558 9

First published in 2006

A CIP catalogue record of this book is available from the British Library.

Printed in China through Colorcraft Ltd., Hong Kong.

For Jamie & Becky, Katie & Jamie & George.

*Who journeyed through the Galaxy with
Dawn & Fizz before anyone else.*

*Never forget the part you all played
in their cosmic adventure.*

Thank you.

1

leaving for good

"Eight hours to go, eight hours to go."

The frizzy-haired girl with the strange, pale eyes repeated these words to herself over and over again as she raced up and down street after street under the early evening sun.

"Just eight hours to go," she panted, wiping the perspiration from her eyes. "Where is she? Where is she!? Only eight hours to go and I can't find her anywhere!"

The frizzy-haired girl stopped on the corner of Parker Street, gasping for breath and clutching the stitch in her side.

"Where … are you?" she panted, as she checked her watch. "Seven hours and fifty seven minutes to go," she said. "Oh this is bad … this is really, *really* bad."

*   *   *

Just a short way from Parker Street and the strange, frizzy-haired girl who seemed to be getting closer to tears as each minute ticked by, a perfectly average girl called Dawn Gray was enjoying being nothing more than perfectly average.

Dawn Gray was a perfectly normal thirteen year old girl. She listened to music and went to the pictures. She had friends and attended school and she had a part-time job, delivering the local paper every Thursday evening.

On this particular Thursday evening, Dawn strolled along the tree-lined street of Wendale Avenue, her curly, mousey blonde hair scrunched back into a pony tail and her iPod thumping away in her ears as she tried to stay focused on her delivery of the Holsum Express.

Dawn hummed and bobbed her head to the music that was filling her mind and thoughts, as she absently ambled down each immaculately paved driveway of each immaculately decorated house and poked a rolled up paper through each immaculate letterbox.

She did not see who was thundering along Wendale Avenue behind her:

- The tall, frizzy-haired girl with the odd, pale white eyes who had been calling Dawn for some minutes from the other end of the street.

- The tall, frizzy-haired girl who was panting to catch her breath and whose brow was glistening, ever so slightly, with perspiration in the late evening sunshine.

The tall, frizzy-haired girl finally caught up with Dawn as she was about to turn, folded Holsum Express in her hand, into the driveway of number twelve Wendale Avenue. The frizzy-haired girl, barely able to breathe, and clutching an agonising stitch in her side, stumbled, lunged and smacked Dawn hard on the shoulder.

Dawn jumped. She screamed. Her in-ear headphones popped out of her ears as she span around, swinging her folded copy of the Holsum Express through the air and landing it, with a crisp *thwack,* on the side of the frizzy-haired girls' ear.

"What … are … you … doing!?" the frizzy-haired girl panted, clutching her ear with the hand that was not already clutching her painful stitch.

"Fizz?" Dawn said looking down at the round figure doubled up in pain in front of her. "What are *you* doing? You scared me!"

"No … time … to explain," Fizz continued to pant. "Come with me … now … have … to go … now." She collapsed to her knees, the ringing in her left ear and the painful stitch in her side becoming too much to bear. "Have to … leave …" she gasped. "… Now … for good … too late … for … anything else … it's started …"

Dawn watched in some confusion and, it must be said, with slight amusement as Fizz completely collapsed on her front, sprawled out in the middle of the pavement.

"What on earth are you talking about?" Dawn asked calmly.

Fizz seemed to find a long gasp of breath from some-where and half turned her head on the pavement to look, bleary-eyed, up at Dawn.

"The end of the world is happening ... tonight," she said.

2

fizz's story

Dawn managed, somehow, to drag Fizz back to her home on Kirkland Street, struggling the whole time to pull behind her the heavy trolley that carried the remaining copies of the Holsum Express that she had, as yet, failed to deliver.

Dawn's mother and father were as accommodating as ever. Mr Gray helped a wobbly but slightly more alert Fizz over to their enormous sofa, while Mrs Gray brought out a tray piled high with plates of chocolate biscuits and glasses of lemonade.

"The sugar will help dear," Dawn's mother said, passing Fizz a plate and a glass.

Fizz, never one to turn down the offer of anything sweet and chocolatey, tucked in and, some three glasses of lemonade and eight chocolate biscuits later, she was ready to explain herself.

"Now then, young Fizz," Dawn's father said, standing himself by the fireplace and adopting his best 'hands on hips' father-figure stance. "What's all this nonsense about the end of the world?"

Fizz was just in the process of finishing her ninth chocolate biscuit: "Buffin' ... boo ... borry babout," she mumbled. "Bor ball bite bafe, Bive babbanged bit ball."

Dawn's dad looked at his daughter in utter bemusement.

"What did she say?" he asked.

"I have no idea," Dawn replied. "I didn't understand a word of it."

Fizz swallowed her chocolate biscuit.

"I said, nothing to worry about. You're all quite safe, I've arranged it all."

Dawn exchanged a puzzled glance with each of her parents. Her mother leant forward and comfortingly patted Fizz's knee.

"Now, what have you arranged dear?" she asked softly.

"Transportation," Fizz said, washing down the chocolate biscuits with another glass of lemonade. "Good bickys, Mrs Gray," Fizz said, once she had swallowed the lemonade. "I'm going to miss chocolate when we leave."

"Leave, Fizz?" Dawn's mother repeated. "What do you mean, *leave*? What do you mean by 'you've arranged *transportation*'?"

"For you all, I mean," Fizz replied, looking around at her hosts and her best friend, her white eyes bright again, her frizzy blonde hair bobbing up and down on her head as though it were full of springs. "It's all in hand, so you don't have anything to worry about."

Again, Dawn exchanged glances with her parents. This time, however, the glances seemed slightly more anxious. It seemed, in all seriousness that Fizz had gone ... completely bonkers.

"Does your mother know you're here, love?" Dawn's mother asked Fizz again, with a gentle tap on her knee.

"Moth ... ? Oh her! Oh, she's not my mother. She was with me when I got here. She's already left!"

There was another concerned glance between Dawn and her parents.

"Maybe we should start from the beginning here, young Fizz," Dawn's father suggested.

"Right, okay, yeah, sure ..." Fizz gabbled. "You're probably all confused aren't you, don't know anything about this do you? No, course not, stupid me, eh? Okay, well, no point in beating about the bush I s'pose, so ... here goes, I'll just cut right to the chase, no messing about, no mucking around ... just the facts, plain and true, just the need to know, that's all ..."

"Fizz," Dawn interrupted. "Get on with it."

"Right, right, 'course, sorry. Get your words out Fizz, you idiot."

Dawn and her parents all found themselves shuffling further away from Fizz the longer she sat on their sofa gabbling to herself.

"O-kay," Fizz took a deep breath and spoke as she exhaled. "The Earth is about to be towed away by the Trygonian Council, in about seven hours and eleven minutes to be exact, for failure to Develop and Evolve Peacefully and Harmoniously in a Co-habited Planetary Environment as outlined in the Interstellar Bill of Co-existence and Harmonious Law and Rights, Section 211-B/3, Sub-chapter Four, The Existence of Universal Organic Life Forms, paragraph six."

Fizz took a huge intake of breath, but before anyone could interrupt her and speak, she was off again.

"The planet Earth will be towed away by a Class Nine Trygonian Council Recovery Vessel. Class Nine, that's the biggest of all the classes ... " Fizz added matter of factly, as if this little detail was suddenly supposed to make everything perfectly clear.

"The Earth will be dumped at the opposite end of your, *immediate* known solar system, somewhere just behind Pluto, where it will receive much less sunlight and will have much less breathable air.

"Now, most of the human race will just fall of the surface of the planet once it is being towed. Believe me, when a planet is re-located, gravity goes crazy; a planet's orbit is disrupted so badly, people just literally fly off the planet and into outer space. But, for those who survive the tow? Well ... due to the lack of oxygen and sunlight ...

they'll all be dead in less than a month, along with every other organic life form on this planet."

Fizz looked around chirpily at everyone. "We all ready to go pack, then?"

3

just the beginning

The evening went on in much the same bizarre and disturbing way and, after having tried to contact Fizz's mother on the telephone and getting no reply, Dawn's parents suggested to Fizz that she stay with them for the evening.

Fizz simply replied that she didn't have any intention of going anywhere anyway, since they all had to be at the same pick up point when the time to leave the Earth came, later on that night. Dawn's parents exchanged yet another, more exasperated, look of concern and bid the two girls good-night.

"Just keep an eye on her," Dawn's mother whispered into her daughter's ear, as she handed her two mugs of hot chocolate and a plate of chocolate digestive biscuits.

"Let her eat. She seems to be calmer and happier when she's eating. Any problems, or if she starts to act ... " Dawn's mother twirled her finger around at the side of her temple, "... funny, just come and give us a call, okay?"

"Okay mum," Dawn replied and headed off up to bed.

In her room, Dawn was surprised to find Fizz sitting cross legged on her bed, still fully clothed.

"There's a pair of my pyjamas there if you want," Dawn said, pointing to a pair of pale blue pyjamas with a picture of a teddy bear on the pocket.

"Thanks," Fizz said, gazing out of the window at the night sky. "They're tempting. I mean, they look comfortable to travel in ... for the journey, I mean - but I think I'll stay as I am."

Dawn opened her mouth to speak but, not surprisingly to her, no words came out. Instead, she just set the two mugs of hot chocolate and the plate of biscuits down on her bedside table and changed into her own pyjamas, pale pink with the same teddy bear picture on the pocket, and climbed into bed.

As she lay there, munching on a biscuit and sipping her chocolate, Dawn considered the evening's events and Fizz herself.

Fizz was a strange girl, everybody knew that. She had come to Keppleton Secondary School last summer, apparently having just moved to the area from far away, (amazingly, Dawn found herself wondering just how 'far away' this was), and it would not be an understatement to say that Fizz had not been well accepted at school.

She was placed in the same class as Dawn and it was Dawn herself who was given the responsibility of looking after Fizz and, as her teachers had put it, making her feel '*welcome.*' Dawn made every effort to make Fizz feel welcome, introducing her to her own friends, helping her find her way around the school and from class to class but Fizz, it seemed to Dawn at the time, had been intent on making life very difficult for herself as well as making it very difficult for anyone else to make her feel at home.

For a start, she dressed peculiarly (not a sin in itself, but when you're wanting to make a good impression you could make a *little* effort to fit in, right?).

Not Fizz. Fizz dressed for every school day in black combat boots, shocking green stripy tights with bright pink shorts over the top, and a black T-shirt which had a rather amusing green alien face on the front and the slogan: I ♥ Aliens.

This image, combined with her wild and seemingly uncontrollable mass of white blonde curls and her peculiar pale eyes, did tend to make Fizz appear somewhat of an outsider.

Her appearance, however, was not the only thing which alienated her from the other pupils at Keppleton Secondary School. Fizz spent her entire time walking around the school commenting on how primitive everything was, from the computers to the very structure of the school building itself. Add to this the fact that she seemed to know everything about every subject (she even seemed to know more than the teachers) and it all made Fizz very unpopular, very quickly.

But, for some reason, against strong protest from her friends, Dawn seemed to stay friendly with Fizz. She liked her in an odd sort of way. Fizz was a breath of fresh air, someone different from the usual array of boys and girls at

Keppleton and, if nothing else, you could always expect an interesting day when Fizz was around.

Yes, Dawn had to admit it, even as she thought about it now … she liked Fizz, which was probably why the pair of them were sharing a room now, Dawn lying in her bed, propped up on her elbow looking at Fizz sitting at the foot of her bed, still gazing starward.

"What's going on with you, Fizz?" Dawn asked suddenly, surprising even herself as she heard her words cut through the silence in the room.

"Huh?" Fizz said, snapping her head round, her blonde hair bouncing gently as she looked at Dawn.

"You having problems at home?" Dawn asked. "I mean … all this stuff you've been saying, it's like … you're making it up to protect yourself from something. And then … not being able to get hold of your mum tonight, have you had a fight or something?"

Fizz just smiled at Dawn but it was not a 'Fizzy' sort of smile. There was no weirdness or kind of 'cute but strange' charm in it; it was a serious, calm, knowing kind of smile.

"You should get some rest," Fizz said softly. "It'll be starting soon. Don't worry, I'll wake you up in plenty of time."

Dawn thought about saying more but decided against it. There was obviously something going on with Fizz but, whatever it was, she wasn't going to or maybe just couldn't talk about it right now and Dawn wasn't about to push her.

Instead, Dawn tossed her half-eaten biscuit back onto the plate (it missed and ended up on the floor), lay back on her pillow and tried to close her eyes … just for a little while.

✵   ✵   ✵

When Dawn awoke, she was so bleary-eyed and so dazed that it took her a moment just to remember where she was, let alone that Fizz was with her and everything that had happened earlier in the day.

It was late, that much was obvious to her, as the sky outside was still black and her bedroom was now in total darkness. She looked down her bed. Fizz was still sitting at the foot of it, only now she was on the edge, her feet planted on the floor. She was still gazing out the window.

"Fizz?" Dawn mumbled, letting her head flop back onto her pillow. "Go to bed, Fizz."

"Don't you go back to sleep," Fizz snapped. "It's just taken me ten minutes to wake you up. I thought I was going to have to bash you around the head with something. It's like trying to wake the dead."

Dawn sat up.

"You woke me up?" She checked the bedside clock. It read 12:07 am. "Fizz, it's midnight, what are you doing waking me up at *midnight*?"

"I told you I'd wake you up in plenty of time," Fizz replied. "We've got twenty six minutes. Here." A small black bag plopped onto Dawn's lap in the darkness. She turned on the bedside lamp and squinted as the bright light blinded her for a second or two. She looked down at the little black bag in her lap, almost too afraid to open it.

"What's this?" Dawn asked.

"Just some things you'll need," Fizz replied, still gazing up at the stars. "It's big enough for everything you have to take and it's got a strap so you can tie it round your waist." Dawn inspected the bag and its strap. "Don't worry, I've made up one each for your mum and dad as well."

Once again, Dawn found her mouth hanging open as she tried to speak, but no words came out. Instead, she thought it best just to unzip the bag and get it over with.

She tipped the contents of the bag out onto her bed.

Inside she found:

- a pair of sunglasses.

- a packet of chewing gum.

- a small bottle of sunblock.

- a small tub of Vaseline.

- a pair of earmuffs.

- and a bright pink swimming cap.

Dawn was beginning to feel a little uncomfortable again.

"Er ... Fizz?" she said, her voice trembling slightly. "What are all these for?" Fizz sighed frustratedly and shuffled down the bed to Dawn.

"I don't really have time to explain all the details of every little thing in here, I didn't think you'd be this fussy. But, okay, I'll have to be quick, there's still a lot to do.

First, I need to explain to you that we're going to be travelling much faster than the speed of light, all right? Now the human body just isn't designed to travel at that kind of speed, it can't withstand the ..." Fizz searched for the right word. "... process or the shock, it would just ... well, dissolve into a pile of ashes. So this stuff is what the experts say will enable an average human being to travel at LX3."

Dawn sat in dumb silence, a sudden feeling of fear and anxiety at being in Fizz's presence washed over her. However, she still managed to mutter ...

"LX3?"

"Light 3," Fizz explained. Dawn's face was blank. "Light speed to the power of 3!" Fizz said. Dawn's expression did not change, Fizz gasped. "Blimey! Light speed times the speed of light, times the speed of light again."

"Oh," Dawn squeaked.

"Right, now ... first, the chewing gum," Fizz began, constantly sneaking glances over her shoulder at the night sky outside the bedroom window.

"The force of travelling at LX3 would knock your teeth right out of your head, so, you chew the gum. That way, your teeth have something to bite down on … other than your tongue I mean." Fizz smiled wryly. Dawn did not return the expression, she didn't really feel like smiling right now.

"Second," Fizz continued. "The earmuffs. Travelling at LX3 … very loud, get it?"

Dawn nodded, her wide-eyed gaze fixed on Fizz.

"Third … the sunblock and the sunglasses. Travelling at LX3 is a very … bright, very hot experience, bad for the old skin and eyes. Imagine sitting on a blazing hot beach in Spain, under direct sunlight all day long and times that by a hundred, get me? These things will protect you.

And lastly, the swimming cap and Vaseline. Travelling at LX3, you always travel headfirst. Now there's a lot of friction and static to endure on the journey, so covering your hair and smothering the swimming cap in Vaseline shoots you through space faster and more smoothly, okay? Now. Questions?"

Millions, Dawn thought to herself, but she could not bring herself to think of a single one. She just shook her head.

"Good," Fizz said and shuffled back down to the end of the bed and continued her star watching. She glanced at her watch.

"Twenty one minutes," she said. "You'd better go wake up your mum and dad."

Dawn couldn't have put it better herself.

Leaving the empty black bag and the other items on the bed, she leapt up and was halfway across her bedroom floor, ready to wake her parents up by screaming and shouting and demanding that this mad, insane, completely bonkers girl was thrown out of the house immediately, when suddenly the most peculiar thing happened.

4

the earth gets towed

It happened in an instant, before Dawn could even really react. All she could do was watch in horror as her wardrobe, the chest of drawers next to it and her bedside table all slid from one end of the room to the other.

Dawn found herself standing at an angle, now looking slightly upwards to her bed and to a very shocked looking Fizz.

"Fizz?" she whispered. "What's happening?"

"I don't believe it!" Fizz bellowed, as she jumped to her feet and vaulted over the bed. "They're early!"

Dawn suddenly felt very wobbly on her legs and her head was beginning to spin, as Fizz began stuffing the chewing gum and sunglasses and all the other bizarre items back into the small, black bag.

"Dawn!" Fizz screamed as she ran across to where her friend was standing, staring blankly into space. "Dawn! Get a grip on yourself will you! Go into the bathroom and splash some water on your face, then … stuff some of this gum into your mouth, smother every bit of skin you have exposed with the sunblock and put the sunglasses, earmuffs and swimming cap on, then cover your head in Vaseline. You got that!?"

Dawn could feel herself getting dizzy, a cold, fainting sensation sweeping through her. All she wanted to do was be sick.

It seemed as though her bedroom was tilting at an angle a little more with every minute that flashed by, and Dawn was struggling to maintain her balance on the uneven bedroom floor beneath her feet.

"Go!" Fizz bellowed, as she turned Dawn towards her open bedroom door and shoved the little black bag with all its contents into her hand. "I'll get your mum and dad!"

But there was no need. Dawn's parents had already come bursting into the room.

"What on earth is going on here?!" Dawn's father shouted, his hands on his hips in his familiar authoritative father-figure style. But, somehow, he did not look so authoritative now, he looked nervous and visibly shaken.

"Bathroom! Now!" Fizz screamed at all three of them. She grabbed another three black bags from the floor at the foot of Dawn's bed and led them all out of the bedroom, down the hall and into the bathroom.

Inside the bathroom, everyone began grabbing hold of something to steady themselves.

"Fizz!" Dawn shouted. "Why is our house tipping!?"

"Tipping?" Dawn's mother said. "We're … *tipping*?"

"We're being towed, Mrs. Gray," Fizz said. "The Earth is being towed away, just like I said it would be. Here." Fizz held out black bags to Dawn's parents. The bags were full of the same things she had given Dawn.

"Wha …" Dawn's father went to say, but Fizz interrupted him before he could finish.

"There's no time to explain!" she screamed. "Any second now, the Trygonian Council Recovery Vessel will begin its journey back across the galaxy and the Earth will be dragged along behind it. And … when that starts … believe me, you wanna be off this rock.

"Now …" Fizz pointed to each item in the black bags, "… chew that, smother yourselves in that, put them on, put that on and smother it in that stuff. I'll meet you downstairs, outside in the front garden in two minutes … don't dawdle!"

Fizz turned to sprint from the bathroom, her own bag of necessities fastened around her waist, but as she flung the door open she turned back.

"And don't forget to tie the bags securely round your waists!"

And with that, the door slammed shut behind Fizz and she was gone.

5

d.r.o.s.s.

It was, to say the least … quite a sight.

Outside the front of number twenty eight Kirkland Street, amidst the immaculately kept squares of lawn, cute little picket fences and numerous brightly whitewashed houses, stood Fizz and Dawn and Dawn's parents, looking, to put it mildly … utterly ridiculous.

Unfortunately for them, most of their neighbours had experienced the same *tipping* effects in their own houses and had come out into the night air to see what was going on (and wondering if they were experiencing some kind of freak earthquake or something).

It only took a minute or so before everyone noticed the Grays standing on their lawn looking skywards, but when they did… there was a deafening roar of laughter from all around.

Dawn was in her pale pink pyjamas and fluffy white slippers.

Her father, in his pinstriped pyjamas and moccasin slippers.

Her mother in an ankle-length nightgown and bright green bed socks.

Fizz was dressed, as peculiarly as ever, in what she had been wearing all day ... black combat boots, stripey green tights, pink shorts and T-shirt sporting its trademark, *I* ♥ *Aliens* logo.

And every single one of them was chewing gum furiously, covered in bright green sunblock, wearing dark sunglasses and earmuffs and sporting a different luminous-coloured swimming cap which dripped Vaseline.

Fizz looked round at the Grays once she realised what everyone else out in the street was laughing at. She looked unsurprised.

"Oh good ... you're ready."

Dawn's father didn't look his hospitable, chirpy self any longer. In fact he spat his words at Fizz through gritted teeth.

"Ready for what ... *Fizz*?" he hissed. "I feel ridiculous."

Fizz, immediately sensing Mr Gray's embarrassment at being laughed at by almost the entire street, tried to ease his concern.

"Oh, don't worry Mr Gray," she said happily. "Not long now, and all this lot who think we look really stupid will be hurtling bum over elbow through the deepest reaches of space, gasping desperately for air to breathe in an oxygenless atmosphere and waiting for their eyes to pop out of their sockets and their heads to burst open. Who'll be laughing then, huh?"

Fizz winked at the Gray family but Dawn and her parents did not get Fizz's little joke.

"Oh I've had about enough of this!" Mrs Gray snapped, and she began struggling to remove her swimming cap. "I will not stand here looking like this, lining up to be a laughing stock in front of the whole street."

"I wouldn't take that off if I were you, Mrs Gray," Fizz warned, but her words of warning were not necessary anyway, as Dawn's mother could not remove the swimming cap due to the vast amount of Vaseline that had been smothered over it.

"Geoff!" Mrs Gray spat, turning around angrily at her husband. "Help me, will you, for Pete's sake!"

"Yes dear, sorry dear," Dawn's father replied, as he began struggling to get his fingers underneath the edge of the swimming cap.

Dawn shuffled closer to Fizz.

"Fizz," she whispered into her friend's ear. "What exactly are we waiting for?"

"Them," Fizz replied quietly, keeping her gaze to the stars. "The Trygonians."

"Oh," Dawn said matter of factly, as though she understood Fizz's answer.

Then she whispered: "Why?"

The laughing neighbours had circled around the lawn, now watching intently as Mr Gray fought to remove his wife's greasy, bright green swimming cap and Mrs Gray battled to remove her husband's luminous orange swimming cap.

Dawn, even though she heard a few neighbours taking bets as to who would remove whose cap first, did not pay them much attention. Her ears, instead, were listening intently to Fizz.

"Because we can't DROSS until we get sight of the Trygonians," Fizz replied bluntly.

"Oh," Dawn replied again, before she uttered "DROSS?"

"Yeah, DROSS." Fizz turned her gaze away from the heavens and met Dawn's eyes. "D-R-O-S-S ... DROSS, Displacement and Restructuring of Outer Shell and Skeleton."

Dawn's eyes squinted in an expression of anger, fear and confusion. She poked Fizz, who had turned her attention back to the stars again, hard in the shoulder. Fizz flinched.

"What?" she snapped.

"I'm gonna need a little more explanation than that," Dawn said, a hint of temper in her voice now. "Call me thick if you want, but due to my current situation ..." Dawn looked down at herself, dressed as she was, outside, in the night-time, in front of every neighbour she knew, "... I think I deserve it."

Fizz hung her head and sighed desperately.

"Oh, okay then. DROSS is the technical term used for transporting people by LX3. Remember LX3, travelling at the speed of light to the power of three? It means breaking your molecules down, zipping them to another point in the galaxy and putting them back together again, okay?"

"Okay," Dawn replied, suddenly feeling on a roll and wanting to ask more. "I didn't understand any of that but I'll take your word for it for now. But why to do we have to wait for the Try ... Traygin ..."

"Trygonians," Fizz finished for her.

"Yeah ... them. Why do we have to wait for *them* to come into view?"

"Because once a planet has been selected for towing and relocation, no-one is allowed to leave or DROSS off. If a planet has been chosen for relocation, it means everyone and everything on that planet at the time has to be relocated with it.

"But, if we wait till the Trygonian Council Recovery Vessel is directly overhead, directly over the top of the Earth, then, for a few seconds, their scanners won't be able to pick up any movement on or off the planet's surface and we'll be able to DROSS off completely undetected."

Dawn was lost, more confused than ever and more than a little terrified. She replied simply with her customary

"Oh."

Behind her, her father had managed to remove his wife's swimming cap and cheers from the neighbours were going up all around them.

"Right," Mrs Gray said, straightening herself up and wiping runny Vaseline from her face. "Dawn, Geoffrey, in the house ... NOW PLEASE!!!"

And then ... it happened.

6

the trygonian council recovery vessel

The light of the moon was suddenly eclipsed, throwing Kirkland Street into an unnatural darkness and stopping Mrs Gray in mid-rant, just as she was about to storm back into the house.

The laughter and jeering from the neighbours all around the front of the Gray's home stopped instantly and everyone's gaze tilted upwards towards the stars.

"Mrs Gray," Fizz whispered softly, her own gaze (though more serious and much less frightened than everyone else's) fixed on the vast shape that was hovering overhead. "I think you would be best advised just to take my word for it and put your swimming cap back on … it's almost time."

This time, there was no further argument; Mrs Gray, her eyes fixed firmly on the staggering, dark monstrosity that was gliding silently above her, raced over to her husband, wrestled her bright green swimming cap from him and began struggling to stretch it back over her head.

The terrifying shape floating over them all was shaped a lot like … a big screwdriver. It spun slowly, its yellow and black striped body rotating against the starlight of the night sky. It made no sound whatsoever. But it did flash: Dawn could see that from the tip of the vessel (what would be the head of the big screwdriver) to its rear (the handle) a pale orange glow was flashing at quick, regular intervals.

From the rear of the enormous screwdriver two floating beams of blue light jetted out, arc-like, making the shape of a rainbow. The floating beams of blue light sprung out and round and down, leading out of sight somewhere miles away.

It took a minute or two for the entire length of the vessel to pass over everyone's heads. A giant luminous sign beneath the back end of the ship flashed a warning which read:

DANGER! VESSEL REVERSING!

And then … it stopped.

It hung there for a brief moment, the giant, dark, screwdriver-shaped thing high in the night sky, up above everyone. It must have been the length of fifty football pitches, yet it didn't emit a single sound.

Slowly the vessel began to upend itself and Fizz scurried to the centre of the Grays' front lawn.

"This is it everyone!" she shouted, as she sat cross-legged on a patch of damp grass. "Come on!"

Dawn and her parents ran to where Fizz was sitting and knelt down beside her. A few of the terrified-looking neighbours spotted what was going on and were beginning to point at the Gray family and whisper amongst themselves.

The giant screwdriver, hovering in the dark night sky above them, came to a halt again. It was now pointing upwards, the tip of the vessel pointing up into the darkness of the night sky above them, seemingly reaching on forever. The floating beams of blue light just hung loosely like inverted rainbows.

Fizz produced something which resembled a firework from her pocket.

Noticing Dawn's quizzical eyes on her, Fizz looked up and smiled.

"It's called an LX-Dome."

Fizz jabbed the LX-Dome into the soft ground and immediately a huge, flat plate of light shot out from beneath it. The disc-shaped patch of light spread out across the grass and slipped itself underneath everyone's bottom. The sensation of sitting on what seemed to be a solid piece of light was quite unusual; Dawn's bottom was getting warmer, but it also felt strangely numb and almost as if it were a centimetre or so off the ground.

At the tip of the LX-Dome a single, scraggly-looking piece of material, like a label, hung out. Written on the label in bold red lettering were the words:

DO NOT PULL!

"Everyone chewing?" Fizz asked. Dawn and her parents stuffed more sticks of chewing gum into their mouths and began chewing furiously. "All got sunblock on? All got swimming caps on?" Everyone nodded. Mrs Gray had, all be it lopsided now, managed to stretch her own swimming cap back over her head. "Earmuffs in place?" Fizz shouted. "Okay ... glasses on."

Suddenly there was a deafening, piercing screeching sound and another single shot of thin blue light bolted out from the very top of the giant screwdriver and darted across the night sky, beyond where anyone could see from the ground.

A few more neighbours were starting to peer at the Gray family, as they sat around in the centre of their lawn. One of the neighbours, a beer-bellied, hairy man called Greg Fawcet, with a purple face and tattooed arms, began marching across the lawn towards the Gray family.

"Hey!" he bellowed, as he stomped across the grass. "What are they up to!? They know something! Hey Geoff, what you up to there? You know something 'bout this that we don't?"

"Oh blimey," Dawn whispered under her breath.

"Who's that?" Fizz asked.

"Our neighbour, Greg Fawcet," Dawn replied. "He's a total idiot."

As Greg Fawcet came closer and closer to the Gray family, an odd and terrifying thing began to happen. The Earth began to roll.

At the same time, the giant screwdriver-shaped vessel in the night sky began moving again, slowly upwards this time.

Everyone screamed.

All of the Gray's neighbours suddenly began falling down in the street; some were sent reeling backwards, some forwards, and some simply plopped down on their knees where they had been standing.

Greg Fawcet, however, was sent hurtling forwards, where he crashed over Dawn and into the centre of the Gray family's little huddle.

"YOU IDIOT!" Fizz screamed at Greg Fawcet. "Shift your fat bum now! COME ON!!! MOVE!"

Fizz suddenly looked horrified as she gazed up at the screwdriver-shaped vessel as it began climbing higher and higher into the dark sky.

The entire street was now angling badly downwards and people were beginning to roll, screaming, down the street and right past where Dawn, her parents and Fizz sat on the lawn, clutching clumps of grass around them to stop themselves rolling away too.

Fizz was struggling to lift Greg Fawcet to his feet, but the man's legs seemed to have turned to jelly and he could not stand up. Dawn and her parents did not help Fizz; they just knelt, in their little circle, now holding hands and looking at each other with absolutely terrified expressions of confusion, fear and more confusion on their faces.

"Oh no!" Fizz screamed, as she continued to try to get the big, tattooed man to his feet. "We're gonna be late … we're gonna miss it … oh no!"

But Greg Fawcet still could not get to his feet. In fact, all he could do was roll around from side to side, his eyes rolling around in his head and his body looking as though it had had all its bones removed from it.

"Oh heck with it!" Fizz finally screamed, as the Gray's neighbour still lay on his back amongst them all, unable to move and now clutching his head and blinking hard over and over again to focus on the big screwdriver that was pulling away further and further into the sky.

"We're out of time," Fizz said, as she looked over the faces of Dawn and Mr and Mrs Gray in turn. "Ready?"

Nobody spoke and nobody moved.

"It'll be over in a second," Fizz said, smiling, as she dropped the sunglasses which had been perched on top of her head down over her eyes. "Here … we … GO!"

Fizz reached down to the piece of tatty paper hanging out of the tip of the LX-Dome. Dawn noticed that its wording had changed. A moment ago, it had read:

DO NOT PULL!

But now it read:

QUICK! YOU CAN PULL NOW!

Fizz grabbed a tight hold of the paper and pulled it hard.

1

travelling at 1×3

A clear dome of light sprung out of the firework and surrounded them all. It looked as though it were made of clingfilm, so they all seemed to be sitting inside a big bubble.

There was a sudden hissing sound … a sucking sound, then there was the peculiar sound of everything seeming to be played backwards. Voices from outside the dome and the sucking, hissing sounds all seemed to be in reverse. Then there was a clear, distinctive *popping* noise and everything went black.

Well … dark … hazy blue to be exact.

Dawn shielded her eyes as brilliant columns of light soared up from the now-dark, void-like ground below her. The columns of light rocketed past her and all around her, up, up, up into the dark night sky above her. The sound was deafening.

She felt her skin starting to burn. It was the strangest sensation, like the tingling feeling on your skin of sunburn, but without the stinging pain. The skin on her face felt tight and brittle, and she had to keep her arm over her eyes to protect them from the blinding columns of light which were continuing to erupt from the ground around her.

Slowly, Dawn managed a squinted gaze around at everybody in the dome with her. Her parents and Fizz were unrecognisable. Their faces and bodies were stretched out and upwards towards the darkness above them; illuminated by the light from the columns, they looked as though they were being stretched like an elastic band.

Greg Fawcet, however, looked completely different.

He looked as though he was screaming out, but it was difficult for Dawn to make him out exactly because he was disintegrating right before her very eyes.

Suddenly, Greg Fawcet reached out and grabbed at Dawn's legs.

"Heeeeeeeeeelp meeeeeeeee!" he bellowed in a strange, eerie kind of echo.

Dawn screamed and slapped and scratched at Greg Fawcet's hand, trying to brush it off.

"Dawn!" Fizz bellowed. "Sit still!"

Dawn grabbed Greg Fawcet's hand and pushed it away from her. She winced as her knuckles brushed one of the columns of light that were disintegrating Greg Fawcet.

Greg Fawcet didn't move. He just lay there, distorted, stretched out like Dawn's parents and Fizz, his hand still outstretched and, with every column of light which blasted up through the dark, void-like ground, a little more of Greg Fawcet disappeared, until there was nothing left of him at all.

Dawn had absolutely no idea whatsoever how long she and her parents and Fizz had been experiencing what was happening to them, but she did know that she was becoming more and more uncomfortable with every passing second.

The bubble-like dome that Dawn assumed they must all still be sitting in was now almost completely full of columns of brilliant, white light; only the spots in which Dawn, her parents and Fizz sat were spared an eruption of light.

But now there were several new things happening to them.

All around Dawn came an ear-splitting whistling sound. It pierced its way through her eardrums and into her brain until, after not very long at all, it was all she could hear. As well as this, the dome had started to rock and bounce. The darkness all around them had gone, and was now replaced by more brilliant white light. It was like sitting in a light bulb.

The dome bounced and bumped uncomfortably for what seemed like forever, pummelling Dawn and causing her to groan out loud every time her bottom left whatever ground there was below her, before she crunched back down again.

She chomped hard on her gum and, as the images of Fizz and her parents dissolved into nothing more than blurry strips of different coloured light, Dawn Gray closed her eyes tight, clenched her fists and hoped … in fact wished … that she would wake up soon.

As it happened, not much more than a minute or so after Dawn made this wish, she did wake up.

The columns of light vanished in a millisecond, as did the brilliant white light all around her. The whistling stopped as well, although it was hard for Dawn to tell straight away because it continued to ring in her ears long after it had actually stopped.

The bumping and rocking beneath her eased slowly and, before she knew it, she was sitting perfectly still, fists still clenched, eyes still squeezed tightly shut.

Dawn unclenched her fists, wincing slightly as she flexed her fingers and rubbed her palms.

She opened her eyes and smiled, relieved to see Fizz standing boldly in front of her: she was removing her swimming cap and tucking her chewing gum behind her ear.

"Hey," Fizz said softly. "How are you?"

Dawn tried to speak but found that her throat was dry and sore and her jaw ached slightly from the gum chewing and teeth grinding she had been doing.

Eventually, she managed a whispered: "O … kay. I … th … think."

"Good, good," Fizz replied, rubbing her knuckles and playing with her fingers absently. She seemed, to Dawn, a little nervous about something.

"Boy ..." Fizz whistled, smiling anxiously. "Have I got a surprise for you."

8

point of departure, point of arrival

It took Dawn all of about five seconds to realise that she was not sitting up in bed and that she had not, therefore, just dreamed the whole terrible experience.

A sudden, cold swell of fear leapt into her throat.

"Don't be mad okay?" Fizz said, still looking more than a little anxious.

The swell of fear in Dawn's throat grew.

"Why … would I be mad?" she asked.

"We've hit a snag," Fizz chuckled nervously.

"A *snag*?" Dawn repeated.

"Yeah, you know … a hitch, a hiccup, a teeny, *tiny* … problem." Fizz made a tiny gap between her finger and thumb to indicate just how small a problem she was talking about.

"I had a terrible dream, Fizz," Dawn said out loud, more to comfort herself than anything else (she didn't really believe it). "Just a little nightmare ... that's *all*."

"Yeah ... well ... not as much of a nightmare as you're about to have," Fizz replied and chuckled nervously again.

It was, funnily enough, exactly at this moment that Dawn suddenly realised that she was sitting, in her pale pink pyjamas and fluffy white slippers, still wearing the bright pink swimming cap, sunglasses and earmuffs, in a smelly, shallow puddle.

How this fact had not come to Dawn's attention sooner than it did is a mystery, but Dawn, beyond any reasonable doubt now, was sure that she had not been dreaming and had not just experienced a terrible nightmare. What was happening to her, whatever exactly it was that was happening to her, was all ... very real.

"Where ... the heck am I, Fizz?" Dawn asked through gritted teeth.

"Well ..." Fizz replied, sighing very matter of factly. "It really is hard to say. I mean, taking into account the trajectory at which we travelled, times that by the speed we were going ... which of course was LX3 ... different kinds of dust and rock particles in the air and in deep space itself which had to be avoided ... otherwise we would have just been smashed into a million, trillion, zillion pieces ..."

Fizz was ticking points off on the fingers on her hands. Dawn, on the other hand, was beginning to turn red with anger as she scrambled and struggled to get to her feet.

"… All that, divided by the number of, according to physicist Gornheim Vilber, infinite different possibilities there actually are out there in the galaxy and …"

"FIZZ!"!! Dawn screamed as she finally reached breaking point. "WHERE ARE WE!!!!????"

Fizz was quite motionless. Stunned into silence by Dawn's sudden, furious outburst, she spoke softly and carefully.

"We're still in your front garden," she said.

For a moment, Dawn wasn't actually able to function at all, neither mentally or physically. She froze where she was, halfway through struggling to her feet. Then it suddenly dawned on her to look around.

She saw nothing she recognised.

There was no lighting for a start. Her street was in total darkness.

All around her were battered, tatty-looking dens lined along, not a pleasant looking avenue or street, but what looked to Dawn to be dusty, dirt tracks. The tatty, rundown-looking dens sat flush next to each other, almost on top of one another. Each den was only a fraction of the size of a house and there were no windows or doors, just roughly-cut holes in the front to get in and out. The holes looked almost as if they had been chewed out of the wood.

All in all, the battered-looking dens looked remarkably like …

"Kennels," Dawn whispered to herself. She looked at Fizz as she finally made it to her feet and straightened up. "They look like dog kennels."

Fizz wasn't paying attention to Dawn; she was looking around, chewing her nails absently, seemingly keeping an eye out for something.

"Uh-huh, kennels, right," she muttered.

"This is not my front garden Fizz," Dawn said, checking herself and making sure she was all there. "This is not my street and that... " she span round and stared at the rotten-looking den that stood where her house had once been "...is not my house. What are you talking about, we're still in my front garden?"

"Oh that's definitely where we are, Dawn. Look."

Fizz produced what looked to Dawn like a straight drinking glass with a light bulb in the end. She flashed it at her friend and Dawn saw that the end of the strange, cylindrical object was glowing orange, and written in small letters on either side of the screen was:

POINT OF DEPARTURE:
DAWN GRAY'S FRONT LAWN.

POINT OF ARRIVAL:
DAWN GRAY'S FRONT LAWN.

"What the heck does that mean?" Dawn asked, as she pulled off her swimming hat and stuffed it into the black bag around her middle.

"This is an LX Travel Coordinate Programmer," Fizz replied. "When you're travelling at LX3, this tells you where you left from and where you have arrived."

"Well, it's broken then," Dawn snapped, pulling her earmuffs down around her neck and shoving her sunglasses on top of her head.

"It's not broken, Dawn. We haven't gone anywhere, well, not physically anyway."

"What does that mean?"

Suddenly, a booming, snarling voice blared from out of the darkness, interrupting Dawn and Fizz's conversation.

"Oi!" The voice growled. "Don't move!"

"Uh … I think it's best that we go now," Fizz said, trembling as she tucked the LX Travel Coordinate Programmer back into her pocket.

"Who was that?" Dawn asked, reading the panic and fear in Fizz's face, and now finding herself absolutely terrified all over again.

"I'm not entirely sure, but I don't think we should stick around here to find out, do you?"

"Stay where you are!" the voice barked. "I'm coming right over!"

"Fancy a late night stroll?" Fizz asked, already beginning to quick-step backwards, away from Dawn.

"Fizz … where are my mum and dad?" Dawn asked, as she suddenly remembered her parents.

"I think we should go now Dawn; come on DAWN! LET'S GO NOW!"

A shadow stretched out in front of Dawn; it was being cast by a figure behind her. She hesitated in turning around to see just who was casting the shadow but, once she had, she wished she had hesitated a little longer.

Long enough in fact to start running, instead of turning around and seeing the six foot alsatian dog that was standing over her.

9

vincent the watchdog

Dawn screamed but, oddly, no sound came out.

So, picture it, if you can: Dawn Gray, thirteen years old, long mousey-blonde hair, dressed in her best pink pyjamas and fluffy slippers, sunglasses pushed up on her head, earmuffs around her neck, covered in sunblock as she stands in a horrible muddy puddle in a dark street, her eyes squeezed shut, her mouth open in an agonising, silent scream, as a six foot dog looks down at her with a look of utter bemusement.

Can you picture that clearly? Good, then let's move on.

Dawn didn't really have time to notice too much about the giant dog before she screamed (silently), turned, scrambled out of the muddy puddle and sprinted as fast as she could after Fizz, down the long, dark, seemingly endless dirt track road.

She dared a glance over her shoulder as she ran, and instantly wished she hadn't.

The giant dog was bounding through the dark after her, snarling and muttering to itself; for every ten steps that Dawn ran, the dog seemed to take only a couple of bounds along behind her … it was gaining on her fast.

An alleyway between two whole towering blocks of the battered looking old kennels appeared to the right and, having lost sight of Fizz a long time ago, Dawn gulped hard, hoped for the best, and turned into the alleyway and into deeper, darker blackness.

Behind her, there was no sound of bounding paws so, for the time being at least, Dawn gave herself a chance to catch her breath, rub her trembling hands together and, once again, scream - this time inside her own head.

As she tried to pull herself together, tried to stop her entire body trembling with fear and shock, Dawn realised that she could hear water running somewhere. A drain, it seemed, was dripping and trickling into a gutter somewhere in the darkness.

Sudden, faint noises made Dawn jump and stare around in the darkness blindly. But she could see nothing. There was no-one to be seen.

Dawn padded down the alleyway apprehensively, breathing softly and shallowly, trying not to make too much noise, trying to keep her wits about her and keeping an eye out in the darkness.

The alleyway smelled foul. It was narrow and cramped. Dawn could almost reach out to the sides and touch both opposite walls, and she could see boxes and bins scattered all around her.

Suddenly there was a deafening CLANG! Dawn jumped back and this time, when she tried to scream, she did manage to let out a tiny but piercing yelp. A dustbin lid rattled and clanged as it span on the ground in front of her, and as she watched the dustbin lid spin Dawn realised that she had backed up against a wall and the end of the alleyway.

Dawn turned this way and that, staring around in the dark, trying to figure out what had knocked the dustbin lid to the ground. Before she even noticed them, Dawn already knew that she was no longer alone in the alley.

There were presences in front of her, moving towards her silently and, although she couldn't see much more than outlines in the darkness, she was sure they were there and she was sure there were several of them.

A ray of clear, misty blue moonlight shot down through the alley as the heavy cloud overhead shifted and, for the first time, Dawn saw what was standing in front of her.

Bulldogs. Six, large, ugly, mean-looking bulldogs. At least, that's what they looked like. They certainly had the heads of bulldogs, but their fur-covered bodies were wrapped up in what looked like dirty bedsheets with holes cut out for the their front legs and heads to stick through. The sheets hung down to the ground, but Dawn could tell quite clearly that the dogs were standing in much the same way that the alsatian had been, on their hind legs, walking very ably and very capably as you or I would.

"Is that … a *human being*?" the brown and white bulldog in the centre of the group said gruffly, as he shifted forward, peering at Dawn, his protruding bottom teeth sticking up over his top lip. He was drooling quite disgustingly.

"I wouldn't believe it if I wasn't seeing it with my own eyes," another of the bulldogs replied.

"It looks … funny," a third bulldog said. "It's … pink and it's got … fluffy feet"

The group of vicious-looking bulldogs began shuffling towards Dawn on their hind legs, their mangy-looking bed-sheets dragging along the ground and scuffing through puddles and mud. They were all drooling uncontrollably and glaring at Dawn horribly through snarled expressions.

"What do we do with it?" the bulldog at the head of the group asked.

Dawn did not wait to hear the answer to this question.

She dashed to her left and leapt up onto one of the tatty-looking kennels, found a foothold and began climbing.

There was immediately a deafening chorus of barks behind her, as she began struggling and scrambling up the towering block of dog houses.

Below her, the bulldogs were frantically leaping up at the foot of the block of kennels and spinning around and around in circles excitedly, as they barked and whined and howled.

Blood pounded in Dawn's ears as perspiration began pouring down her face, stinging her eyes. The tower of kennels did not feel at all stable and, as she climbed higher and higher up, feeling the painful stab of splinters in her feet through her fluffy slippers, she winced, grabbing a hold of sharp bits of old wood with her hands, trying to steady herself on the structure that was already starting to tilt backwards slightly.

Oh no! Oh please ... NO! Dawn screamed in her head.

She was completely unable to comprehend what exactly it was that was happening to her. In the grand scale of things that had happened so far this evening, this was by far the worst. But, somehow, the whole LX3 thing, the giant alsatian and the bulldogs now jumping around and howling some twenty feet below her just wouldn't seem to make themselves feel real in her brain.

Through the darkness, blindly feeling her way, Dawn climbed and climbed, higher and higher, leaving the howls of the bulldogs more and more faintly behind her. She had no idea where she was going and no idea what she would do once she was there, but, she figured, the top of the tower of battered, tatty dog kennels would have to end somewhere and, once she was at the top and safe (from the bulldogs at least), she would work out her next move, if there could even be one.

And then, the tower of kennels staggered. Dawn gripped whatever she could manage as tightly as she could but the tower continued to sway backwards.

The bulldogs began to howl more and more excitedly below her as they watched their human prey wobbling high above them. They waited for the tower to give way and for Dawn to come hurtling back down to the ground to become an easy meal.

There was a cracking sound.

Dawn's foot slipped beneath her and she jolted as the weight of her body was suddenly thrown onto her outstretched arms. And there she was, suddenly hanging by her fingertips, with, some thirty feet below her, a pack of mutant and very, *very* hungry bulldogs.

The tower of kennels wobbled again; there was another, more deafening crack from somewhere in the centre of the structure, then the whole thing suddenly gave way.

Dawn squeezed her eyes shut and waited for the end … *her* end to come.

But, amazingly, she did not fall.

Instead, she suddenly felt a strong, warm, fuzzy grip around her wrist and then, in the blink of an eye, she was heaved up onto some kind of platform, onto which she was thrown down and left, collapsed on her back and staring up, once again, at the alsatian.

Dawn wanted to scream, but she had tried that before and nothing had happened. She wanted to run but she knew there was nowhere to run to. Instead she just lay there staring up through the dark night sky at the alsatian's face.

The dog was black and grey with wisps of silvery fur around its temples and where its whiskers began. It did not look threatening any more, nor did it look like it was about to attack her.

"Are you alright?" it said.

Dawn paused for a moment, not sure exactly how she should answer a six foot dog which had just saved her life but which could, potentially, be eyeing her up as a late night snack.

"Uh … yeah … er … I think so," she replied in a whisper.

"Good, good, then." The alsatian was surprisingly well spoken; if Dawn had not seen what it was that was talking to her, she could have easily thought that the voice belonged to some polite old English gentleman.

"Here, allow me to help you back to your feet, young lady."

Dawn felt the same warm, fuzzy paw around her back as the alsatian shuffled her to her feet where she stood, still craning her neck to look up at the dog.

"Allow me to introduce myself," said the alsatian. "My name is Vincent. Class 1, Guardian Watchdog around here. And you are?"

Dawn blinked deliberately trying to clear her mind.

"Dawn," she mumbled. "Dawn Gray."

"Nice to meet you, Dawn Gray. You are a very lucky human. You do realise that, do you not?"

"I suppose I am," Dawn replied. "Those bulldogs were just about to …"

"Eat you," Vincent finished for her. "Yes, they would have done. Extremely unpleasant bunch, the bulldogs, no sense of manners or etiquette. I mean, is that really any way to greet a guest to these parts?" Vincent scoffed and sniggered. "I do not think so."

Vincent removed what seemed to be some kind of holster from his back, adjusted his dirty-looking bedsheet, which was a little better fitting than the bulldogs' and had obviously been arranged to look a little more like a uniform, and plopped himself down on the ground, which, Dawn now saw, was some kind of walkway which ran between the tops of two tower blocks of kennels.

Vincent sat like any dog would, his front legs out in front of him, his hind legs beneath him, and surveyed Dawn properly, whilst cocking one of his hind legs up and scratching himself behind the ear.

"So," he said calmly, "since human beings have been extinct for over two hundred years now … would you mind telling me how you came to be in my neck of the woods, Dawn Gray?"

Dawn opened her mouth to answer but, suddenly she saw behind Vincent a familiar figure shuffling along towards her.

Fizz trudged past the big alsatian without even acknowledging he was there, and collapsed on the ground next to Dawn.

"All right?" Fizz said casually. She had her swimming cap back on, as well as her sunglasses and earmuffs, and she was chewing frantically. But she looked exhausted, she was sweating and there were a few cuts and scratches on her face.

Dawn just glared at her: "Oh, I'm great," she snapped. "You?"

"Fine," Fizz replied bluntly, as she removed another of the firework thingys from a strap around her green tights and stood it on the ground in front of herself and Dawn. "'Scuse me," Fizz said to Vincent.

"Not at all," Vincent said, getting to his feet. "Do carry on."

The scraggly-looking piece of material hanging out of the firework read:

OKAY YOU CAN PULL NOW!

Fizz looked at Dawn: "Sunglasses?" she said matter of factly.

"Fizz, what is going on?"

Fizz just held her hand up to shush Dawn.

"Sunglasses?" she repeated.

"Fizz!" Dawn protested. "Tell me what's happening, will you?! What's going ... !?"

"Put your sunglasses on!" Fizz snapped. She was obviously tired and a little bit touchy.

Without another word of protest, Dawn sulkily removed her sunglasses from the bag around her waist and put them on.

"Earmuffs?"

Dawn put them on.

"Swimming cap … Vaseline?"

Dawn stretched her cap on and rubbed Vaseline all over it.

"Gum?"

Dawn produced three sticks and stuffed them into her mouth.

Fizz pulled the piece of material.

The bubble-like dome shot up all around them.

Dawn managed to mouth a '*Thank you*' to Vincent, who was standing outside the dome watching them knowingly, before he vanished in a bolt of white light.

The columns of light shot up from the ground all around Dawn and Fizz.

It was all happening again.

10

kevin
the flying rugby ball

The columns of light disappeared again, the bumping settled down and the ear-piercing whistling stopped, leaving Dawn's ears ringing. Again, she found herself in darkness.

She got to her feet a little more quickly and more steadily this time and immediately found Fizz, looking happier and much more satisfied now.

"Ah, now this is better, this is more like it, this is right, we're all right now."

An overwhelming desire to cry, shout, stamp her feet and punch Fizz hard on the nose swept over Dawn.

"Are we!?" she screamed. Fizz jumped out of her skin and began shushing Dawn.

"Keep your voice down will you!" she hissed. "We don't want anyone to know we're here now, do we?"

"I don't know," Dawn snapped. "Where are we supposed to be, Fizz? Where are we now? What's happening to us? What's happened to the Earth? My street? My house? My neighbours? And where the heck are my mum and dad?"

"All right," Fizz said, smiling coolly and plopping herself cross-legged on the cold, hard ground. "You're right, you deserve an explanation."

Fizz got as far as: "Well ... the thing is ..." before a small door opened with a hissy kind of *pfssst* sound and a square of light appeared through the darkness.

Dawn watched as a shape hovered and moved towards them through the air.

The object was in the shape of a rugby ball and it spun towards Dawn and Fizz, giving out a rather eerie green glow of light which illuminated everything around them. Dawn could now see that there wasn't actually much to illuminate. In fact they seemed to be standing in the middle of a big, empty warehouse.

The flying rugby ball reached Dawn and Fizz and stopped spinning. Suddenly, a pair of shutters zipped up on the robot's shiny silver body, revealing two friendly little blue eyes.

"Good evening," it said in a rather pleasant, metallic kind of voice. Dawn and Fizz were both amazed to see another shutter zip open on the robot's face, opening a cheerful smile of light.

"My name is Kevin and I will be your guard for the durwation of your journey to the bwidge which will be appwoximately seven minutes. Please do not panic, do not wun along any of the corwidors which I will be leading you thwough and please do not, under any circumstances, twy to escape."

"*Twy* to escape?" Fizz repeated.

"Pardon?" the robot replied quizzically.

"You just said, please do not *twy* to escape," Fizz said. "Don't you mean … *try* to escape?"

"That's what I said," the robot replied cheerfully. "Please do not twy to escape." Fizz grinned to herself.

"Okay," she said. "What happens if we do *twy* to escape?" Dawn was surprised by Fizz's coolness in asking this question but, she had to admit, she was a little curious to hear the answer.

"Pardon?" Kevin said again, his little, glowing blue eyes seeming to glaze over slightly and go a little paler in colour.

"If we try to escape," Fizz repeated herself. "What happens?"

"Er …" the spinning, rugby ball-shaped, flying robot called Kevin looked utterly perplexed.

"… Ummmmm … well, I don't weally know actually. Isn't that funny? No one's ever asked me that before and nobody's ever twied to escape, so I have absolutely no idea."

"Fizz," Dawn whispered out of the corner of her mouth. "What's going on?"

Fizz shushed Dawn with a gentle, discreet wave of her hand.

"So … let's just say, for argument's sake, I tried to escape now … What would you do, Kevin?" Fizz smiled at the robot as she waited for him to answer.

"Well … that's a twicky one," Kevin the robot chuckled to himself. "Nothing I suppose. You want to twy it?"

"Twy what?" Fizz said. "I mean … *try* what?"

"Escaping," Kevin said.

"I wouldn't even know where to escape to," Fizz admitted.

"Well, I would suggest, that is to say if anyone should feel inclined to make an escape attempt, that the best course to take would be to use the escape pods." Kevin span and his eyes flickered happily.

"The escape pods?" Fizz said. "And … where would these escape pods be?"

"Level fifty nine," Kevin replied agreeably. "Weapons hold, interplanetawy passport contwol, laundwy level and escape pod access."

Dawn had a headache.

"And how would I get to level fifty nine?" Fizz asked, shuffling closer to Kevin and giving his shiny, metallic body a friendly pat.

"Lift from the bwidge, or down the escalators from any corwidor exit. I'll show you all the ways down to level fifty nine on our way to the bwidge. Shall we go?"

"Please … lead on, Kevin," Fizz smiled.

The little robot span around and began whistling cheerily to himself as he headed back out of the vast, dark room and towards the square of light from which he had just hovered.

Fizz and a rather confused and headache-stricken Dawn followed.

The ship's maze of corridors seemed to stretch on for miles. Apart from a few, circular porthole windows, nothing but black and rusty silver piping surrounded Dawn and Fizz as they shuffled along behind Kevin, who was spinning and whistling happily as he led them to the bridge. His whistling echoed all around them, bouncing off and around the vast, circular, pipelined walls of the corridors.

"You were about to explain to me what was going on," Dawn snapped softly to Fizz as she pulled off her swimming cap, earmuffs and glasses and stuffed them into her bag. "You were, I hope, about to tell me just where the heck my mum and dad are?"

"Oh right, yeah, of course." Fizz began, as she removed her own accessories. "Well, we are currently aboard the Trygonian Council Recovery Vessel, the one we saw hovering above our heads just before we hit LX3 on your front lawn. See?"

Fizz stopped for a moment by one of the porthole windows and pointed through it. Dawn followed Fizz's finger out into the vast, awe-inspiring blackness of space. Far below and behind them, attached by the floating beams of blue light, the planet Earth was tumbling and spinning along. Dawn felt her stomach turn ... her home planet was indeed being towed like a worn-out old car.

"What are we doing here?" Dawn asked. This was just the first of a million questions currently zooming through her tired brain.

"We're waiting till the ship is a safe distance from the atmosphere the Earth was once in, and then we're going to DROSS on down to Squetania Blib."

Dawn felt her headache worsen.

"Seq ... Sqee ... what?"

"Squetania Blib," Fizz repeated. "It's a beautiful place. The locals are friendly and very open to immigrants; we'll be able to settle happily there."

This response of course did not answer any of Dawn's immediate and, she felt, urgent questions. But she sensed that they only had a short time before they reached the bridge and, whatever was going to happen there, she guessed that they would not have the opportunity to talk very much in private, so she pushed for as much information as she could in the short time they had.

"And my mum and dad?" She asked quietly. "Where are they?"

"Safe," Fizz replied.

"Safe?" Dawn gasped. "What does that mean ... safe? Where are they?"

Fizz said nothing.

"Fizz? Where are my parents?"

"I'm not sure," Fizz said bluntly. "But don't worry, I get a lifeline readout on my handset." Fizz gestured to the straight glass with a bulb in the end sticking out of the back pocket of her shorts.

"The LX3 Travel Coordinate Programmer. It tracks the life forms that made the jump to light speed with us. I'm getting their vital signs readout and it's good and strong. Once we're settled on Squetania Blib, I'll sort out a way to get them to us."

Dawn supposed that Fizz was trying to make her feel better about the whereabouts of her parents but, not surprisingly, she didn't.

"And what about just now? The dogs, the alsatian, all that ... What was that?"

"Oh that," Fizz scoffed. "That was nothing ... a mis-calculation. My mistake, don't worry about it."

Dawn was just about to lunge at Fizz and begin choking her for more information other than the stupid, vague answers she was currently giving her, when Kevin the robot stopped at a giant steel door.

"Here we go ladies," Kevin chirped. "Best smiles on, just be nice and all will be well. Give me a call when you're done and I'll show you those escape pods."

"Thanks Kev," Fizz replied cheerily, as the giant steel door zipped up silently and disappeared into a slot in the ceiling. "See you in a minute."

Fizz and Dawn walked inside.

11

jowlox the one

"Tell me this isn't happening," Dawn said. She didn't know whether to laugh, cry, scream or just collapse in a heap on the floor.

The bridge was not entirely dissimilar to the warehouse Kevin had found them in. That is to say, it was exactly the same. It was huge and vast … extremely dark and damp with odd puddles on the floor and there was absolutely nothing in it.

Nothing, that is, except for the ridiculously oversized black swivel chair that was being swivelled from side to side by … a little girl.

"Kill me," Dawn whispered. Fizz looked at her, stunned.

"What did you say?"

"Use some sort of ray gun or something," Dawn went on. "I'm sure you must have one. Go on … vapourise me, melt me, whatever it is that ray guns do. I've had enough of this now. It's just getting silly."

"You're the one being silly," Fizz replied, smirking. "Ray guns indeed. You crack me up."

"SILENCE!" A booming voice exploded from within the darkness of the bridge.

Dawn and Fizz both jumped out of their skins and skipped from foot to foot anxiously as they peered around, trying to figure out where the voice had come from. It only took a few seconds before they both realised that it had come from the little girl.

The little girl had the sweetest face. Rosy cheeks, a button nose that was ever so slightly upturned and a flowery hairband which pushed her blonde locks away from her face.

She sat, swamped in the enormous black leather chair. She was wearing a lilac gingham dress and her little legs dangled from the edge of the leather chair. She was wiggling her pink shoes in front of her, kicking at the air - out of what seemed to be boredom.

"My presence disturbs you?" the little girl said, peering through the darkness towards Dawn. Her voice was child-like now, but there was a calm, adult air of menace about it. She did not speak like a little girl.

"Uh … me?" Dawn said, jabbing herself in the chest with her finger.

"Yes … you," the little girl replied. "My presence disturbs you, it seems. Is this so?"

"No … no, not at all," Dawn replied, feeling a little uneasy about being put on the spot by a child. "It's just … I

wasn't expecting to see a little girl sitting here, it just …
surprised me, that's all."

"What would you prefer?" the girl asked quite bluntly,
as she crossed and uncrossed her ankles and fidgeted in her
seat.

"I … don't … really know."

"Be careful how you answer," Fizz advised her quietly.

"I suppose I didn't know what to expect," Dawn
finished.

"This is a humanoid form is it not?" the little girl asked,
genuinely.

"Pardon?" Dawn replied.

"The form I am currently in." The little girl looked
down at herself. "This is a humanoid form, yes or no?"

"Well … yes … it is, yes." Dawn was eyeing Fizz, who
was trying not to make eye contact with her but was still
mouthing the words *Be careful* to her silently.

"Then why do you feel so uncomfortable?" the little girl
pushed.

"I tell you what," Dawn said with a sudden spark of
confidence in her voice.

She was getting the hint from Fizz's warning and
thought it best if she just dropped the subject of her feeling
uncomfortable altogether.

"It was a shock, that's all. But now we're talking, you and me ... I'm fine with the situation. A little girl on the bridge of a giant space ship - what could be more natural? Good luck to you and all that."

"I can adopt other forms if it helps you," the little girl said, as she hopped down from the giant leather chair and scurried over to Fizz and Dawn. "Whatever you want, really."

"It's fine, thanks," Dawn replied. "You just stay as you are there. I'm totally comfortable with you."

"You're sure?" The little girl asked.

"Positive." Dawn replied.

"Certain?"

"Absolutely."

"Because ... if you want ..."

"Hey, what's your name anyway?" Fizz interrupted the little girl before the conversation got any more confusing.

"Jowlox," the girl replied, looking down at her shoes and scuffing the toes shyly along the floor.

"Jowlox?" Dawn repeated.

"Jowlox the One," the girl added.

"The one what?" Fizz asked.

"The *only* One," the little girl explained. "I'm the only Mimicaabus left, the only of my kind alive anywhere in the galaxy."

"Mimi-what-us?" Dawn said.

"Mimicaabus," Fizz explained softly. "A species who replicates or mimics anything."

Fizz turned to the little girl, Jowlox, who was smiling up at them sweetly.

"So how d'you get *this* gig, Jowlox?"

"Gig?"

"Well, you're flying a Trygonian Council Recovery Vessel aren't you? A vessel which happens to be towing the Earth, right? How come the Trygonians hired you? I thought they just hired freelance Likk-lax."

"Licklacks?" Dawn repeated.

"Likk-lax," Fizz corrected her. "L-I-K-K, dash, L-A-X. Likk-lax. Kind of a breed of big, dumb stupid thugs who happen to be very good at driving tow ships and who don't demand a huge pay cheque."

"Oh." Dawn felt her thick, pounding headache coming on strong again.

"Oh, the Trygonians didn't hire me," Jowlox replied, grinning to herself mischievously and looking down at her shoes again.

"They didn't?" Fizz sounded surprised.

"No." Jowlox leant in a little and began to whisper. "I stole this ship - and I've stolen the Earth." She fell about in a fit of child-like giggles. Fizz's face dropped and she turned a horrible shade of white.

"What does she mean … *stole* the Earth?" Dawn whispered, but Fizz shushed her with a wave of her hand again.

"What are you talking about, Jowlox? You *stole* this ship and you *stole* the Earth?"

Jowlox's giggles stopped. "I'm the last of my kind, I told you. There are none like me left anywhere in the galaxy. So, I thought, why not steal myself a whole new planet, a whole new home? Adopt the form of the inhabitants of that planet and go live there, blend in, become one of them. My race was designed to live in other forms, so it wouldn't be hard to do and I could begin a new life with a whole new species on a whole new planet."

Fizz couldn't move, her jaw hung open.

Dawn's expression was similar. Although she didn't know as much about Mimicaabusses and Likk-lax, she understood the basics of what Jowlox had just said to them.

"And where are you taking the Earth, then?" Fizz finally found enough voice to ask.

"Back to where my planet once was," Jowlox replied, skipping around the dark, vast room now and singing happily in-between her answers. "My world was sent out of its own atmosphere by a jolt from a Star-tempest."

Dawn looked at Fizz but she didn't even have to ask. Fizz knew straight away what Dawn was going to ask.

"A Star-tempest is like a hurricane or tornado in space, only fifty million times more powerful. The most powerful ones can knock an entire planet off its own orbital axis and send it spinning off into deep space, which is what little Jowlox here is saying happened to her planet."

"As it span through space my planet, my home, was sucked into a black hole … I've never seen it since," Jowlox finished.

"And where were you when this happened?" Dawn asked, feeling proud of herself that she was understanding enough of the conversation now to contribute to it.

"Holidaying on Ibanix 3. When my shuttle returned home I just floated around space for a month before I realised what had happened."

"And you intend to stick the Earth in the gap where your planet used to be," Fizz said aloud, just to clear things up in her head. "Keep the physical form you're in now - humanoid form - then beam yourself down onto the planet's surface and hope you just … *blend in*?"

Jowlox clapped her hands excitedly and skipped around some more.

"That's right. Pretty neat idea, huh?"

"Yeah, pretty neat," Fizz lied. "Listen, Jowlox, that robot that brought us here, Kevin. Is he yours?"

"Yep, all mine. He was the only service droid aboard this ship when I stole it. Isn't he cool?"

"*Really* cool," Fizz replied, clapping her hands along with the little girl and even skipping a little herself. "Do you think you could call him in? I'd love to play with him."

Jowlox opened the giant steel door with a push of a button and then screamed, like a spoilt child, for Kevin.

Kevin glided into the darkness of the vast bridge, whistling and spinning chirpily, his glowing blue eyes shining brightly in the gloom.

"Hey Kevin," Fizz said, as he came to a spinning halt in front of them all. "Wanna show us where level fifty nine is now?"

"Okey dokey," replied Kevin and span away from them, leaving Dawn and Fizz to follow him towards the lift.

12

explanation time

"Where are we going!?" Dawn cried, as the lift shot down at the speed of a bullet.

"Level fifty nine," Kevin replied chirpily. "Weapons hold, interplanetawy passport contwol, laundwy level and escape pod access."

"Yes, yes, I get that bit," Dawn said frustratedly. "I'll put it another way shall I? What are we going to do when we get to level fifty nine?"

"We're going to get the heck off this ship," Fizz snapped in response. She seemed agitated and more than a little keen to make a sharp exit from the stolen Trygonian Council Recovery Vessel they were currently standing on.

"Stop!" Dawn cried out loud and, with a spine-shuddering jolt, the speeding lift came to an abrupt halt, surprising Dawn (who hadn't actually expected the lift to do as she told it to) and sending her and Fizz crashing to the ground.

"What are you doing!?" Fizz screamed, as she moaned and groaned her way back to her feet. "This thing is voice-activated!" Dawn winced slightly as she rubbed her back, pulling herself to her feet.

"I didn't know that, did I!?" she shouted angrily.

"Tell me what's going on, Fizz! Right now. The alsatian, this thing, Jowlox up there, why we're leaving so soon, where my parents are, everything, right now! If you don't, I'll keep telling this lift to stop every time you start it again. Get me!?"

Fizz puffed her cheeks out and sighed heavily, sensing (quite rightly) that she was cornered.

"'Scuse us a minute, Kevin," she said politely.

"Oh, don't mind me," Kevin replied happily. "I'll just wait over here and whistle along to myself." He span around and floated over to a corner of the lift, facing away from Dawn and Fizz and, true to his word, began whistling happily.

"Okay," Fizz started. "But I'm gonna be quick explaining all this, right? I wanna get off this ship quick smart, so you better just keep up with me and follow what I'm saying, okay? 'Cause I'm not gonna back track and explain in detail any little points you don't quite understand or little snippets of information you weren't listening hard enough to get. Got it?"

"Okay," Dawn said, taking a deep breath and preparing herself. "Go for it."

It is noteworthy, at this point that you, the reader, also follow closely the following explanation as it will hopefully clarify just exactly what the blazes is going on.

"When the light dome went up on your front lawn, just before we hit LX3, that idiot neighbour of yours, Mr Fawcet, caused a disturbance in the light flow."

"I'm lost already," Dawn said.

"I told you not to interrupt me!" Fizz bellowed. She composed herself again and continued.

"The light travel columns were broken and our paths were separated. By 'ours' I mean yours and mine and your mum and dad's." She took a breath.

"Now, travelling at LX3 is tricky and a lot of things can go wrong and some big, fat lump of an interfering neighbour can really muck things up.

Basically, at LX3 you can travel one of three ways. One, your physical being can travel to another point in the galaxy very, *very* quickly. Two, you can actually travel to an alternative dimension and three, you can travel backwards and forwards through time itself."

Fizz paused, giving time for her friend to interrupt her again just so she could shout at her, but Dawn remained silent.

"Your parents are somewhere in the galaxy, that much I'm sure of." (This little bit of information did not reassure Dawn one bit.)

"But they're in another time, another dimension maybe. I've located them, but it will take a while before I can get them to us … mainly because we have to be somewhere safe before I can do that.

"The alsatian and all that was at exactly the same spot as where your house stood, but it was a very, very long time in the future. Again, we have Mr Fawcet to thank for that little blunder. I managed to recalculate our journey back into the LX Travel Coordinate Programmer and get us back to the right place and the right time ... here, on this ship."

"So why are we leaving now, then?" Dawn asked.

"Because I thought there were going to be Likk-Lax aboard this thing," Fizz replied. "They wouldn't care if anyone was stowing away on board. They probably wouldn't even have ever known. Likk-Lax usually just sleep for the entire duration of a journey.

"The plan was just to shoot you, me and your parents far enough at LX3 to get us off Earth and onto the nearest, safest, stable environment, which was the ship that was towing the Earth. We'd be safe, we wouldn't stand a chance of falling off the face of the planet as it was being towed and, once this ship passed a safe, stable, nice looking little planet, i.e. Squetania Blib, I was going to DROSS us all back down onto the surface and we could all live on our new planet happily ever after."

"But?" Dawn asked, sensing that Fizz's story wasn't quite over yet.

"But, I didn't take into account the fact that the Trygonian Council Recovery Vessel we were going to stow away on was going to have been stolen by some power mad, insane little girl! Jowlox is mad as a hatter and I for one do not want to be stuck on a ship with him, her, it - whatever it is - longer than I absolutely have to! So we're gonna take

these escape pods and take our chances on the first habitable
-looking planet we find. Good enough for you?"

Dawn nodded. She couldn't really think of anything to
say.

"Good," Fizz said. "Can we go now?"

Dawn nodded again.

"Hey Kev!" Fizz exclaimed. Kevin span away from his
corner and stopped whistling immediately.

"You called?" he beamed happily.

"Level fifty nine," Fizz demanded. "No more inter-
ruptions, let's just go!"

13

level 59

The lift stopped again, this time much more smoothly … there was almost no jolting at all.

The doors hissed open and Kevin span excitedly out into, this time, a brighter room.

"Level fifty nine," he chirped. "Weapons hold … "

"Yes, yes, we know," Dawn snapped, cutting Kevin off.

As they walked out into the brightly lit and cheerful-looking blue and white room, Dawn gazed all around her at the series of flickering neon signs which hung from the ceiling, high above her head.

A blue neon sign read:

WEAPONS HOLD.

KEY HOLDERS ACCESS ONLY.

A flashing pink neon sign read:

INTERPLANETARY PASSPORT CONTROL. PLEASE HAVE APPROPRIATE PAPERS, ID AND APPEARANCE REPLICATORS READY.

ANY SPECIES SPORTING MORE OR LESS THAN ONE HEAD, TWO ARMS OR TWO LEGS MUST DECLARE ALL ADDITIONAL LIMBS AT THE CHECK-IN DESK.

A third neon sign, this one flickering red and green, read:

LAUNDRY SERVICES.

PLEASE CHECK POCKETS FOR ALL COINS (LOCAL OR FOREIGN) AND LASER WEAPONS.

"'These the escape pods, Kev?" Fizz's voice whispered from somewhere behind Dawn.

Dawn turned to see Fizz standing inside what looked like … well, I have to be honest, it looked like just a great, big, green jelly bean.

"Corwect," Kevin said, as he hovered over to Fizz and joined her in the strange-looking giant sweet.

Dawn wandered over and climbed into an escape pod next to Fizz. It looked as though the jelly bean had been sliced open up the middle and the top half flipped open. It was just big enough for one person. There were no controls or dials, buttons or switches of any kind: it was just big, long, and green.

"It's a bit rubbish isn't it?" Dawn said, as she stepped gingerly inside the big jelly bean.

"It twavels at gweat velocities," Kevin replied, spinning with enthusiasm for the pods. "They weally are wonderful things. They twavel almost as fast as LX3 itself and will deposit its occupant on the nearwest, safest habitable planet in the nearwest, convenient solar system."

"Cool," Fizz said.

And then Dawn made a terrible mistake.

She lay back, down on the floor of her jelly bean, testing it for comfort. And, instantly, the 'lid' shut down and locked itself.

"Oh dear," Kevin whispered, his blue eyes expressing what Fizz could have sworn was a look of concern.

"What just happened!?" Fizz bellowed, as she looked at Dawn's escape pod beginning to smoke and rattle and tremble.

"The pods are activated by movement and pwessure," Kevin replied. "The moment one sits down, the movement and pwessure of the ... buttocks activates the device."

"Is Dawn about to be shot out into space!?" Fizz screamed.

There was a terrible *Zzzzziiiiiiip!* sound and, in the blink of an eye, the escape pod Dawn had just sat down in … disappeared through the floor.

"Yes," Kevin replied happily. "She is."

14

fizz's plan of action

"Where did she go!?"

Kevin just looked at Fizz, the light on his face, where his mouth should be, upturned at the corners like a little, innocent smile.

"Kevin! Where did Dawn go?"

"Go?" Kevin beamed, his blue eyes twinkling. "I'm not sure I understand the question?"

"You're not sure you understand the question!?" Fizz repeated. "The escape pod! The one my friend was just in, right there, right next to this one, right next to us! Where-did-it-GO!?"

"It was deposited," Kevin replied matter of factly.

"Deposited? Deposited where?"

"The nearwest habitable planet," Kevin said.

"Which was?" Fizz asked.

"Oh … I couldn't answer that I'm afwaid. The course is pwogwammed automatically by the escape pod the moment its occupant sits down; the destination is undetermined until that time."

"Right," Fizz said suddenly, deciding on a plan of action in her head. "Let's go."

"Go?" Kevin span excitedly. "Where are we going?"

"Wherever my friend went," Fizz replied.

Suddenly, silhouetting itself against the bright light of the open doorway, a towering, monstrous figure loomed. Its shadow was ghastly as it cast itself over the open, brightly lit interior of the escape pod. Fizz felt her blood run cold and a sudden jolt of fear leapt up into her throat.

She looked up, across the room outside her escape pod and saw what she could only think to herself was a … great … big … enormous …

"What … is … that?" Fizz gasped slowly, as the indescribable shape oozed its way across the floor towards her. Kevin turned himself around, casually.

"That is Jowlox," he said. "Jowlox the One."

"I thought Jowlox the One was a little girl?" Fizz asked, slightly confused.

"That was Jowlox the One's physical interpwetation of a human being, that is how Jowlox intends to find acceptance once he has settled himself on his new home … the Earth. Jowlox can, in fact, assume the physical appearwance of most anything he wants."

"And … what is he now?" Fizz stared across the floor at the shape squelching and squidging its way towards her.

It was about the size of a hot air balloon, soft pink in colour. It rolled across the floor, the creases and crevices of its fat, sloppy skin squishing against the hard floor. And all over the surface of the gigantic, soft pink, blancmange-type thing were hundreds and hundreds of pairs of bright red lips, each of them making disgusting smacking and slurping noises at Fizz.

"That is Jowlox the One's interpwetation of what your species and many other species, including Earthlings, wefer to as … a hug."

"Oh," said Fizz calmly. "Is that what it's supposed to be?"

"Indeed," Kevin went on politely, gazing with his intense blue eyes at the enormous, squelching, lip-smacking blob as it slimed its way across the floor towards them.

"In his naive attempt to entice you to stay, Jowlox the One has manifested himself as what he has interpweted to be the ultimate symbol of love and welcome … a hug."

"That is his interpretation of a hug?"

"Jowlox the One is incapable of defining or expwessing physical emotion or, for that matter, explaining it or understanding it," Kevin explained. "Therefore, his only means of cweating an emotion or an act of love or fwiendship is to manifest it physically. This is what he has come up with."

Fizz sighed deeply.

"So … you're telling me …" she began, "that because Jowlox has realised that we're trying to leave this ship …"

"Yes," Kevin interrupted.

"He … is attempting to persuade me to stay by offering me love and … lots of hugs and kisses, apparently."

"Yes."

"… He has created … that sweaty, drooling, slimy-looking blob." Fizz finished.

The blob was indeed now drooling quite uncontrollably.

"Jowlox the One has been alone for many centurwies," Kevin explained. "His determination to persuade you to stay and accept him and love him and take him as one of your own is great."

"Yes … yes, I can see that," Fizz said, as the slurping sounds coming from the blob grew louder and the thing itself squelched closer. "Anyway," Fizz said smiling at Kevin. "Shall we go?"

"Go?" Kevin said sounding, for once, genuinely confused. "Go where?"

Fizz lay back in her own escape pod. She grabbed a hold of Kevin and pulled him down onto her as the lid shut down.

If Kevin was startled and angry with what Fizz was doing, he did not show it. Instead, he chose to spin around excitedly and make strange kinds of *whooping* noises.

Fizz waved at the blob through the hazy, thin slits in the jelly bean escape pod which acted as windows.

The 'hug' seemed to be screaming and wailing despondently. It was almost a heart-breaking sound.

"To find Dawn," Fizz said triumphantly.

Kevin stopped spinning.

"That won't be possible, I'm afwaid," he said softly.

The blob outside had reached the pod and was attempting to crack the outer shell with an alarming number of wet, slimy kisses.

"What?" Fizz said. "I thought you said this thing would deliver us to the first habitable planet it came across?"

"It will," Kevin concurred.

"So that'll be the same planet Dawn's on then."

"It would have been two minutes and eleven seconds ago. The ship has moved, at a gweat speed, some distance in that time and, I'm afwaid to say that the first habitable planet we come acwoss now may well be some considerwable distance, in light years I mean, away from the planet your fwiend is on."

The noises of the squelching, squidging blob sliming its way all around the outer shell of the pod and slobbering it with slimy, disgusting kisses was deafening now and, to add to it, alarm bells were ringing in Fizz's head. She felt, and not for the first time in the last few hours, like she was about to just pass out. But, as she knew full well, she was already lying down and there wasn't really enough room in the escape pod to collapse and fall over anyway.

"Great," Fizz said sarcastically.

Zzzzziiiiiiip!

The pod was gone.

15

the galaxy inn

Galaxy Inns really are the most remarkable places and have to be seen, experienced and stayed in to be believed. The biggest and most extravagant of all the Galactic Hotels, they are often visited by some of the most important and famous beings in the galaxy.

The particular Galaxy Inn in question here is situated on the very rim of our solar system in the *Carpai* sector.

It was, at the moment when what appeared to be a giant green jelly bean crash-landed just outside its main entrance, just about the most exciting place in the Galaxy to be.

The hoards of different beings from around the galaxy who were crowded around the outside of this Galaxy Inn barely even noticed the enormous jelly bean as it hurtled, skidded and screeched to a halt just a few feet from the hotel's main doors.

Everyone was too busy looking up at the large, blue, flashing sign above the hotel's doors, which read:

THE GALAXY GUYS

PLAYING TONIGHT AT THE GALAXY INN

FOR ONE NIGHT ONLY!

The crowd didn't even move a muscle as the strange, rather shaky-looking figure dressed in weird pink clothes staggered past them and into the hotel's main foyer.

The main entrance hall to the grand and exquisite Galaxy Inn hotel is quite simply … dull.

The walls are white, the décor is white. The floor, the ceiling, the lights, the checking-in desk: everything is completely pure white and very uninteresting.

The reason for this is that Galaxy Inns, unlike hotels we have here on Earth, cater for somewhere in the vicinity of twelve thousand different species from around the galaxy, some of which do not travel very well at all and become extremely homesick.

The problem of making every guest at a Galaxy Inn feel welcome and at home, regardless of their origins, species or race, was solved some time ago by a chap called Professor Grobblepot the eleventh.

Professor Grobblepot the eleventh (the eleventh in a long family line of a species called Genuous) created a device called the Optical Comfort Replicator, or OCR. The basic function of an OCR is to copy the visual look of an individual's home planet.

OCRs, you see, have a built in scanner which reads a wearer's visual memory of their home planet. The OCR can then project this visual memory back out onto the blank, pure white surroundings, giving the wearer the feeling that they are on their home planet.

Genius really.

True, there have been a few minor cases of brain scrambling, brain shrinking and even complete and total brain melting, but let's not dwell on one or two (or even a dozen) isolated cases.

The OCR truly is a miracle of space-aged technology and, even as Dawn Gray was strolling through the main foyer of the Galaxy Inn, a million miles of space and time from home and completely unaware of where she was or how exactly she got there, with her OCR on, and an image of home displayed all around her, she was beginning to feel a little better.

The clerk at the checking-in desk smiled up at Dawn as she approached and, much to her surprise, he looked decidedly ... human.

"Hello, Miss," the clerk said chirpily. "Checking in?"

"Um ... I'm not sure," Dawn replied shakily.

"Well, if you're checking in, I'm afraid we really are full unless you're prepared to share with another guest. Are you prepared?"

"Prepared for what?"

"To share."

"Um … I don't have any money. Sorry." Dawn turned the top pocket of her pyjamas out to prove her point.

"Mun-ny?" The clerk repeated uncertainly. "What is *mun-ny*?"

"To pay you … for a room I mean. I can't pay you to stay here."

The clerk smiled again.

"I'm sorry Miss, I'm not sure I understand. You do not *pay* to stay at a Galaxy Inn."

"You don't?"

"My goodness no!" The clerk roared with laughter. "The civilised galaxy hasn't used any such crude ways for aeons! Nobody uses the process of payment for things any more! In fact, the only planet I know of that still uses such a vile, degrading form of exchange is Earth."

The clerk suddenly eyed Dawn suspiciously. "You're not an *Earthling* are you?"

Dawn felt sweat instantly on her brow, and her stomach span wildly.

"No," she replied, managing to keep her voice from trembling. "Of course not, I'm a ... Vulcan."

She had no idea why she said it, she had never even really watched an episode of Star Trek. It was just the first thing that came into her head.

"*Vulcan?*" the clerk repeated. "I've not heard of ... Vulcan. You're not from the newly formed Zirtoz Republic are you?"

Dawn, of course, knew that she had no choice other than to answer ...

"Yes. Yes I am, that's probably why you've not heard of Vulcans before."

"Ah well, that explains it then," the clerk smiled to himself as he pulled out from under the desk a strange-looking item resembling a CD, except that it seemed to be made entirely of light.

"There are so many new republics and factions since the old Zirtovia disbanded, I struggle to keep up with them all. Zitovs, Zirtovians, Crysalia, Strumbiks ... *Vulcans*, it really is too much."

"Pardon me for saying," Dawn said, interrupting the clerk. "But you look a little ... *human* yourself."

"Oh don't!" the clerk exclaimed, horrified. "You think I'm not completely ashamed to resemble that disgusting species, even slightly!? Goodness gracious me ... the resemblance has been the plague of my people for more years than I can remember. Thank goodness for these, eh?"

The clerk pushed his little wheely chair back from the desk to reveal quite the most astonishing sight Dawn had ever seen and, by this point, that was *really* saying something.

The clerk had no legs. Instead he had a mass of wild, slithering roots; hundreds of them all seeping out of the skin at his waist and each of them clutching and grabbing onto things to hold him up and move him around.

"Being purely organic … *literally* organic is the one feature we have to prove to people that we really aren't humans. From the waist up there's no telling, but as soon as we reveal our LifeRoots people look at us in an entirely different and, I might add, a whole lot more friendly light."

Dawn could say nothing. She simply smiled politely.

"Anyway … here's your Room-Ray." The clerk plopped the CD of light directly into Dawn's hand; it felt warm but also completely solid.

"Room number 3065, floor 58. You can take a Flowboard to your room. I believe you'll be sharing with a Yinka; very pleasant species. Just be sure not to … well, you know what I mean, not to stare. They can be a little bit … funny about their appearance."

"They look strange or something?"

"You've never seen a Yinka before?" Dawn shook her head.

"No, I haven't, sorry. Should I have?"

"Oh my. Well … well, they're a bit difficult to describe just remember … don't stare and you should be fine."

"O-kay," Dawn replied, still a little uncertain of what she was just about to get herself into.

"You'll be attending the performance, I assume?" the clerk added.

"The performance?"

"The Galaxy Guys, here ... tonight, one night only." The clerk was suddenly completely delirious with excitement.

"They really are just the hottest boy band around in the galaxy at the moment and they won't be in this sector for another millennium. You'll kick yourself if you don't see them now, because the next time they play here they'll be over two thousand years old and, well, let's face it, probably past their best."

"I'll be sure to pop in and catch the show, then," Dawn replied politely.

"Very good, Miss. Enjoy your stay at the Galaxy Inn and remember ..." The checking clerk suddenly put on a totally forced and well-rehearsed smile. "You may be light years from home but the light in our home is always burning brightly ... for you."

"Er ... thank you," Dawn replied as she walked away from the desk. "Oh and er ... live long and prosper and all that," she said, wishing immediately that she hadn't.

16

arthur
the intergalactic tax man

There were no checking-in problems for Fizz on the planet where her escape pod landed.

In fact, all in all, Fizz couldn't have hoped for a better planet. It was lush and green, and had a constant source fresh water which came from a stream which seemed to run through the very centre of the entire planet. And the trees and plants grew hundreds of different tasting fruits and vegetables.

The planet was completely uninhabited for most of the time, and it even had its own twenty five foot outdoor cinema screen showing all the latest movies, which it picked up from satellites orbiting close by.

Oh yes, and Fizz even had the good fortune of being escorted out of her escape pod by a rather dashing man in a pinstripe suit and carrying a briefcase.

The man was tanned and tall and handsome and he was extremely charming.

"Are you okay, Miss?" he asked, as Fizz stumbled, trying to find her feet.

"Yeah, yeah, fine … I think. Who are you?"

"Oh, I'm an Intergalactic Tax Collector." The man held his business card out to Fizz. "Arthur, that's my name."

He smiled as he pointed to the bit on the card where his name was written. "Arthur, that's me. Arthur the Intergalactic Tax Collector."

Fizz handed Arthur back his card, cautiously. She had heard about these creatures, these … Intergalactic Tax Collectors. These beings travelled across the known and unknown galaxies searching out people who owed money in taxes.

"So what are you doing here, then?" Fizz asked warily.

"Looking for you," Arthur the tax collector grinned.

"Why?" Fizz asked.

"Because you're the first one I could find," Arthur replied mysteriously.

Suddenly, a spinning lump of metal drifted up from the inside of the escape pod and Fizz suddenly remembered …

"Kevin!" she called out, as the flying rugby ball span and turned in the air, his shiny body gleaming in the daylight, his blue eyes staring around wildly and excitedly.

"Is this … ?" Kevin stuttered. "Is this … the … *outside*?"

Fizz looked puzzled.

"The outside?" she said, scrunching up her nose. "The outside of what? You mean the ship you were on?"

"Yes … YES!" Kevin exclaimed. "I have been a service dwoid on that ship since I was constwucted some two hundwed and thirty eight years ago … I have never been able to leave it. All I have seen of the west of the galaxy is what I have been able to observe on scanner scweens and monitors. Is it!'"? Kevin bellowed.

"IS THIS THE OUTSIDE!'"?

Arthur looked bemused.

Fizz, on the other hand, looked very pleased with herself; she felt a sensation of warmth and satisfaction wash over her. She was glad to be able to bring so much joy to something, even if it was an annoying, spinning, rugby ball-shaped machine.

"Yes Kevin," she said softly, patting the little robot on the side. "This … " she paused for dramatic effect and opened her arms wide gesturing to everything around her. "… is the *outside*."

Kevin suddenly span around and faced Fizz. His eyes faded from blue and began to glow a menacing red. Steam began to flood out of him.

"Well what are we doing here you MORWON!!!!!?????" he bellowed. His outburst was so startling that it actually sent Fizz toppling backwards into Arthur the tax man who, himself, was cowering from the terrifying, rage-filled robot.

"I mean what are we doing here!!!??? Are you MAD!? I've been locked up in the same ship for the last two hundwed and thirty eight years and you come along and suddenly decide that I need a little holiday to some off world planet, some … some … alien wock.

"Think of the diseases we could be exposing ourselves to here! Think of the … of the … of the potential danger around evewy corner. There could be monsters, wobot-eating monsters around evewy corner, oh the danger, oh doom, doom, DOOM!

"I can't handle this, I can't handle the exposure to outside elements, I was safe on my little ship … my home … the only place I ever knew! What were you thinking, what were you … ooh, ooh look!"

Kevin's eyes suddenly faded back to their placid pale blue as he spotted something fluttering around in the air behind Fizz.

"It's a *LEAF*!" Kevin screamed and zipped off in pursuit of the fluttering bit of greenery.

Fizz stood a moment in stunned silence, until Arthur drew her attention back to the matter in hand.

"Could we … ?" He gestured to the notebook and pen he was holding.

"Yeah, sure," Fizz said absently, still staring after Kevin, who had caught the leaf and was in the process of rolling around on the lush, green ground cuddling it and giggling wildly.

"You travel a lot Miss … " Arthur went on.

"Fizz," Fizz replied.

"Miss Fizz?" Arthur said.

"That's right."

"You travel a lot then, Miss Fizz?"

"Loads."

"Last destination?"

"Well, unofficially, my last destination was some weird alternative dimension where dogs ruled the Earth and I was nearly savaged and killed. But I was only there five minutes, so I suppose that doesn't really count. Before that, my last destination was the Earth."

"*The* Earth?" Arthur said, jotting the name down in his notebook and raising his eyebrows. "Nice place."

Fizz laughed.

"Bit crowded though," Arthur added.

"Not any more," Fizz said under her breath.

"Not any more?" Arthur repeated, looking up at Fizz from his notebook.

"Don't worry," Fizz said, waving her comment off with her hand. She figured that eventually everyone would find out that the Earth had been towed to the dark end of space; it wasn't her right to tell the story.

"Okay," Arthur continued. "And where's your friend?"

"My friend?"

"Uh …" Arthur looked in his notepad to find the name he was searching for. "Miss Dawn Gray?"

Fizz froze. She was suddenly aware that there was something definitely not right with Arthur the intergalactic tax man. In fact, there was something most definitely *very wrong* about him.

"Dawn Gray?" she repeated. "Never heard of her."

Arthur smiled knowingly and straightened his immaculate tie.

"Oh really," he said. "Come now, Miss Fizz. I know you were travelling with her. Just tell me where she is. This has nothing to do with you; I just need to speak with Dawn Gray."

Kevin's wild, ecstatic giggling was niggling at Fizz's ears and she turned to see that the little robot had abandoned the leaf and was now giddily zooming along the ground, chasing what looked very much like a squirrel up and down a tree.

"Is he alright?" Arthur asked.

"I'm not really sure," replied Fizz. "I thought he was, but now I'm thinking he's a little on the unbalanced side."

"The unbalanced side of what?"

"Sanity," Fizz replied coolly. "Listen, honestly, I don't know where Dawn Gray is. We got separated; that's why I'm here with the mental, flying, giggling toaster over there."

Arthur seemed to contemplate Fizz for a moment and then he smiled.

"Okay, I'm gonna believe you … for the moment," he said. "But don't be surprised if I come back and see you very soon."

Arthur the intergalactic tax man produced what looked to Fizz like a pen from his pocket. He held it out in front of him and clicked the top twice. Instantly, a clear shield of light appeared and encased Arthur inside it.

"Dragornus Six, please," Arthur said.

"Wait!" Fizz exclaimed, suddenly realising that Arthur was about to perform some kind of DROSS manoeuvre and beam off the planet. "Why are you looking for Dawn!? Who sent you to find her?"

"Who sent me?" Arthur replied. "Her mother and father of course."

"Her mum and dad!?" Fizz cried out in astonishment. "You know them?!"

"Of course I know them," Arthur replied. "Everybody in the galaxy knows King Mistagray and Queen Missesgray."

In a bright flash of white light, Arthur was gone, leaving Fizz stunned and standing on the lush green planet alone.

Then she heard an insane giggle behind her. Kevin was still playing chase with the squirrels, and she remembered that she wasn't exactly alone.

17

binka the yinka

Dawn's Flow-board whizzed and glided upwards like a rocket-fuelled skateboard.

Flow-boards are quite the most dangerous things ever invented. (They were created, by the way, by the same man who came up with the OCR, Professor Grobblepot the eleventh.)

They look like skateboards, but they work and move in a completely different way. Flow-boards have no wheels, they simply … float or flow through the air.

Every Galaxy Inn has a rack of Flow-boards next to the checking-in desk. A guest selects a board, places it on the floor and steps onto it. Immediately, the Flow-board is activated, rises off the ground and begins to hover.

However, the Flow-board becomes dangerous when one tries to move it. Flow-boards glide in the direction their riders walk, so, if you want to go forward, you simply walk forward and the Flow-board skids you along. It turns right when you turn right, it turns left when you turn left and it stops when you stop.

The problem with Flow-boards, however, is they have no acceleration control. Its rider could walk in the direction they want to go at nothing more than a slow amble or stroll but the Flow-board they're riding will fly along at ten times that speed.

The basic idea of the Flow-board is very clever indeed. It is intended to get a guest to a spot only they can direct it to, but at ten times the speed and with no extra strain on the rider's legs.

However, Flow-boards send more people flying off, leaving them sprawled on Galaxy Inn foyer floors all over the galaxy, than they do gliding them to their rooms. That is why so many people, even if they have two hundred and ninety nine flights of stairs to climb to get to their room, choose to walk rather than take a Flow-board.

Dawn Gray, however, was not aware of the dangers of Flow-board travel, at least, not until it was too late.

As her Flow-board flew over staircase after staircase, Dawn found herself gasping for breath. She was running as fast as she could aboard the Flow-board, just trying to keep up with it, as it zoomed her to her room.

The staircases twisted up and up, passing floor after floor and bizarre-looking creature after bizarre-looking creature, until the Flow-board flew off onto floor 58.

"HEEELP MEEEEEEEE!" Dawn cried as her Flow-board flew down the corridor. It sped past rooms *3045*, *3047*, *3049*, *3051*, *3053*, and Dawn felt her legs starting to give way beneath her. The faster she ran to keep up with the Flow-board, the faster it travelled. It was quite the most unnerving mode of transport she had ever been on.

3055, 3057, 3059, 3061.

Dawn knew there was nothing else for it. Her room was approaching and, as yet, she had absolutely no idea how to stop her Flow-board … she would have to make a jump for it.

3063 …

She saw it, *3065*. Dawn threw herself, eyes squeezed shut, heart racing, into the air. She felt a thud in her back and head as she slammed into the wall and slumped, in a heap, on the floor.

The Flow-board came to a perfect, cushioned, comfortable stop the second Dawn left it.

Dawn looked up at the harmless-looking hovering skateboard from where she lay, crumpled on the floor, feeling completely useless and hugely embarrassed.

"Oh, I get it," she whispered to herself as she pulled herself to her feet and tapped the Flow-board lightly with her fingers. It just wobbled in mid air. Cautiously, she raised a fluffy-slippered foot and tapped her toe against the surface of the Flow-board; it bucked and jolted like a coiled spring waiting to jump. Dawn nodded her head.

"I've got you sussed," she said to herself. "Down!" She commanded, not really expecting anything to happen but, to her amazement, the Flow-board floated to the ground like a feather, where it lay completely motionless. Dawn smiled to herself.

Am I the coolest or what? she thought proudly, thoroughly satisfied that she had been able to train her Flow-board all by herself.

Dawn Gray picked her Flow-board up off the floor, slipped it under her arm and removed her Room-Ray from her pyjama pocket.

There was a very obvious slot in the door to room 3065, into which the Room-Ray was to be inserted. Dawn dropped the solid CD of light into the slot and the door to her room zipped open.

She stepped inside.

*   *   *

It wouldn't be true to say that Dawn was surprised by what she saw as she stepped into room 3065. She was by now, as I'm sure you can understand, beyond surprise.

At first glance, Dawn could only see her reflected memories of home, through her OCR. The London Eye turned slowly toward the back of her room, her house on Kirkland Street stood in the foreground, bathed in sun and surrounded by border upon border of roses and chrysanthemums.

Dawn's stomach lurched. How she missed home. All around her, reflected off the white surface of her room, were memories of home ... of Earth. Rivers gushed past, Big Ben chimed in the distance, ducks quacked, cows mooed and cars honked their horns. Dawn suddenly felt tears welling up in her eyes as the thought of never seeing her home again suddenly invaded her mind, reminding her of the reality of her situation.

But then she noticed it. In the centre of her room, amidst all her sights and sounds of home, was a great, big, talking … bottom.

Forgive me for dropping that last little point in so abruptly. It was done in order to give you some idea of the shock Dawn actually felt when she herself saw the great, big talking bottom.

She pulled off her OCR and the room immediately turned to brilliant, pure white, but the big, talking bottom remained.

The figure in front of Dawn was tall. Dressed in a black, sequined robe which hung to the ground, covering every last inch of its body, it stood, arms folded up in front, hands slipped into loose sleeves which hung to the being's waist. The high collar of the figure's outfit was circular and sticking up, way past its neck, (if it, indeed, actually had a neck to speak of), and there, right on top of the collar was a smooth, pink bottom.

The crevasse down the middle of this bottom, was twitching and moving, as though it were speaking and, either side of it, two dark eyes stared piercingly at Dawn.

"You must be … the Yinka?" Dawn asked nervously. She had never talked with a bottom before.

"I am Binkaliach Morstrak and, yes, I am of the species Yinka-leelak-taknivadaar. Greetings."

Dawn struggled to hide her smile.

"So you're name's ... Binka then?"

"In short. Yes."

"And you're a ... Yinka? That right?"

"Correct."

Dawn bit down hard on her lip to prevent a laugh escaping.

"So you're ... Binka the Yinka then?"

There was a silence between them, a silence which suddenly made Dawn wish she could stop smirking - but she could not.

"Please do not stare," Binka the Yinka replied finally. "It is extremely rude and offensive. I am quite aware of my appearance and the ... shall we say ... amusing qualities of my name and species. Would you care for a drink?"

Well ...

Dawn thought,

... how can I refuse a talking bottom?

18

quizzel the galaxy guide

Quizzel was a legend amongst his fellow Galaxy Guides; a legend, in fact, throughout the known galaxy.

He was the first of the Galaxy Guides. That is to say, he was the founder member and the brains behind the organisation which was *The Galactic Association for Galaxy Guides and LX Travellers*.

It had been over three hundred years since he had founded this organisation and, in that time, Quizzel and all subsequent Guides, whom he had *personally* interviewed and to whom he had assigned the prestigious post of Galaxy Guide, had helped somewhere in the region of seventy three billion life forms relocate to other planets, for one reason or another. It was a record and a reputation that Quizzel was proud of.

He had always had absolute and total faith in The Galactic Association for Galaxy Guides and LX Travellers … until now, that is.

Now, the future was looking bleak for Quizzel and his team of Guides. Now Quizzel found, for the first time in three hundred years, that he was seriously considering retirement.

His organisation had made a mistake. In fact, his organisation had made such an almighty, huge mess of things that the galaxy was heading for a disaster of such enormous magnitude that The Galactic Association for Galaxy Guides and LX Travellers could well be shut down and all of its members rounded up and exterminated, unless Quizzel managed to sort the mess out before anyone noticed that the galaxy's space-time continuum had been cut in half and was actually about to implode into one humungous black hole.

Quizzel landed his flashy, shiny silver ship on the surface of the lush green planet and immediately disembarked. On his way down the gang ramp he was stunned to be greeted by a rather annoyingly happy-looking flying robot.

"Hello!" the robot said, hovering close to the middle of Quizzel's three purple heads. "What are you?"

"Get out of my way," Quizzel's left head snapped.

"And mine," his right head spat. As Quizzel strode past the robot, his third head spun around and stuck his tongue out.

The robot sped after Quizzel, anxious to make conversation.

"You've got thwee heads," the robot chirped.

"Very observant of you," Quizzel's middle head (the head which generally did most of the talking) replied sharply.

"Did he just say thwee?" Quizzel's left head asked.

"I think he did," his right head replied. "What's thwee?"

"You're purple," the robot went on.

Quizzel ignored the robot as he trudged into a heavily wooded area not far from his ship. Birds were singing cheerily in the trees high above his heads, a bright pink sun beamed down through the treetops and the woodland all around Quizzel was a spectrum of brightly coloured plants, fruits and flowers. It really was stunningly beautiful ...

It made Quizzel feel quite sick, the mood he was in. He was not in the mood for beautiful things.

"I like your hair," the little flying robot continued, as it gazed up and down the long mane of hair which flowed down the back of each of Quizzel's three heads. "It's just like a girl's hair."

Quizzel span round on his heels and produced a weapon which resembled a water pistol with a tennis ball on the end. He aimed it at the hovering robot in front of him.

"Do you know what this is?" Quizzel growled.

"It is ... a ... Dissolverwiser." The robot stuttered.

"No it's not," Quizzel snapped. "It's a Dissolveriser."

"That's what I said," the robot argued. "A Dissolverwiser."

"No you didn't," Quizzel's left head said. "You said ... Dissolverwiser."

"What's a Dissolverwiser when it's at home!?" Quizzel's right head asked.

"Enough!" Quizzel interrupted, turning his gaze to the little robot. "Robot, do you know what it does?"

"Well, I, personally, would have thought the name spoke for itself, weally. I mean ... Dissolverwiser ... ? Dissolve ... ? I mean, you don't have to be a genius to work it out do you, after all ..."

"DO YOU KNOW WHAT IT DOES!" Quizzel bellowed angrily, his scream echoing around the forest silence and sending the birds flapping from the trees above him.

The robot made a strange, metallic gulping sound.

"It ... dissolves things."

"It dissolves ... *anything*," Quizzel pointed out. "Including metal, do you understand?"

The robot said nothing but tipped himself forwards and back in a kind of nodding motion. Quizzel took this to mean that he understood completely.

"Good. Now ... kindly leave me in peace, or I shall be forced to prove that it does, in fact ... dissolve *anything*, *including* metal."

Quizzel turned away and continued on his way through the forest. The little robot hovered away in the other direction, muttering to himself.

"I was only going to ask your name," he babbled softly. "I just wanted to let Queen Fizz know that we had a visitor."

Quizzel stopped dead in his tracks and spun around to face the robot again.

"What did you say?" he hissed, all three of his heads glaring at the robot. "The name ... just then ... who did you say?"

"Queen Fizz," the little robot repeated.

"*Queen* Fizz?" Quizzel repeated.

"Well, technically, she's not weally a queen, far fwom it to be honest with you. It's just that there's nobody else on this planet to tell her that she can't be queen so she's decided that that's what she wants to be ... a queen. Queen Fizz. It's a joke if you ask me but ... "

"Shut up!" Quizzel interrupted. "Take me to her, NOW! Take me to this ... *Queen* Fizz."

19

fizz's whole lot of trouble

The second Fizz saw who was with Kevin, she jumped so high that she catapulted herself out of the hammock she had been lying in for the best part of the last five days.

"Qui ... Quiz ... Quizzel ... ?" she stuttered.

"Sir!" Quizzel bellowed as he stomped towards Fizz. "If you please, you may be holidaying here, number eighty five, but The Galactic Association for Galaxy Guides and LX Travellers still has a ranking system and you will follow it when you address me."

"Yes ... sir ... sorry ... sir," Fizz said. "Sir ... do you really have to call me that?"

"Call you what?" Quizzel replied.

"Eighty five," Fizz answered. "I really don't like it. It makes me sound ... well, a bit thick really."

"How many Galaxy Guides are there in The Galactic Association for Galaxy Guides and LX Travellers, eighty five?"

"Eighty five," Fizz replied, knowing, straight away, that the argument was lost.

"And, who is the most recent addition to the Galaxy Guides? Who is our newest member?"

"Me."

"So you are number … ?"

"Eighty five." Fizz scuffed her foot along the ground like a sulking child.

"So … therefore, you are known as … number eighty five. Really, I can't be expected to remember the names of every Galaxy Guide I've hired in the last three hundred years, can I?"

"No sir," Fizz mumbled beneath her breath.

"Anyway, eighty five," Quizzel continued, "I have absolutely no interest in what you are doing lazing about here sunning yourself on a planet you have absolutely no right to be on, so I'll come right to the point."

"Straight to the point," Quizzel's left head echoed.

"Ooh, you are in *sooo* much trouble," Quizzel's right head laughed. Quizzel himself, however, looked very serious.

"The space-time vortex has been disrupted," he said gravely.

Fizz stared at Quizzel with a blank expression.

"Is that possible?"

"It is possible, eighty five, because you made it possible." Quizzel replied. "Your attempt to DROSS the Earth girl and her family from Earth before it was towed was … how can I put it … a complete disaster."

Fizz immediately protested.

"Ah, now, sir, that wasn't my fault. There was this bloke, right? This bloke called … what was his name? Fawcet, that's it, Greg Fawcet. And he tried to jump into the LX-Dome just as we were about to DROSS off and he mucked everything up, and … "

"Silence!" Quizzel interrupted. "The details do not concern me, number eighty five. What concerns me is that your stupidity has … "

"Brace yourself for this," Quizzel's right head interrupted.

"This is unbelievable," his left head added.

"Will you two shut up!" Quizzel bellowed to his two extra heads.

"Sorry," they both said together.

"Your stupidity has ripped a hole in the vortex … in space and time itself."

Fizz stared at Quizzel in dumb silence. She wasn't sure she got it.

"O-kay," she said softly. "And that's bad is it?"

Quizzel's extra heads giggled.

"Bad!?" Quizzel screamed disbelievingly. "*Bad*!? Number eighty five, the galaxy is about to destroy itself! Don't you understand that?"

Fizz's face was blank. Obviously ... she didn't understand.

"The galaxy, eighty five," Quizzel continued to explain. "Space and time ... is full of a million and one alternative dimensions, and in each dimension an entirely different future is played out.

"Why, as we stand here speaking right now, somewhere, out there ... " Quizzel gestured upwards towards the reaches of space above them, "there are hundreds, thousands maybe even millions of other Quizzels and number eighty fives living out different lives and different futures.

"Do you understand what I'm saying?"

Fizz had the same dumb expression on her face.

"Er ... I think so," she said. "Different dimensions, different futures. Right, that would explain the dogs."

"Indeed it would, yes." Quizzel replied. Fizz looked amazed.

"You know about the dog planet?"

"Of course I do," Quizzel replied with a smile.

"We know everything about every Galaxy Guide," his left head said smugly.

"We monitor you all very closely," his right head added.

"The dog planet you arrived on was Earth in a very distant, very different, future. An Earth from a different dimension. You should not have been there. You had absolutely no right to be there. On that Earth, human beings are extinct. Can you imagine what those animals must have thought, seeing Dawn Gray … ?"

"Well, I suppose it must have been a bit of a shock," Fizz replied, matter of factly.

"I'll say," Quizzel said. "How do you think Dawn Gray would feel if she was sitting in her back garden one day and a dinosaur peered over the fence?"

Fizz smirked.

"That'd be funny," she said. "I'd love to see that. Dawn would freak!"

"It most certainly would *not* be funny, number eighty five!" Quizzel snapped.

"Now Dawn Gray is in the wrong dimension … in the wrong time in the wrong bit of the galaxy. The space-time vortex is there for a reason, number eighty five. Space and time is separated into different dimensions for a reason. In Earth's dimension, man landed on the moon in nineteen sixty nine but in one of Earth's alternative dimensions, the moon was destroyed by a meteor shower twenty five years before that. Do you understand what I am saying now?"

Fizz looked blank again.

"A bit," she said uncertainly. "Dimensions and space and time and all that stuff. But I have to say, sir, I'm still a bit confused."

"Thicko," Quizzel's right head said.

"Now I can see why she ripped a hole in space. If she had another brain cell she could be a meteor."

Fizz sneered at Quizzel's extra heads.

Quizzel moved slowly to Fizz and, gently, almost fatherly, he took her hand in his and smiled at her.

"I'm going to explain this as simply as I can, eighty five, okay? You must understand … this is important. The galaxy is full of space and time, and space and time is divided into different dimensions. It is very complicated and very precise, like an old Earth clock. A clock is made up of hundreds of tiny little parts that, together, all help to make it work.

"But what happens if one … *just one* of those tiny little pieces is taken out?"

Fizz wasn't sure whether this was a trick question.

"It stops working?" she said uncertainly.

Quizzel smiled.

"It stops working," he repeated.

"Dawn Gray is like a missing cog from a clock. She is in the wrong place in the galaxy, in the wrong space and time. She is somewhere she should not be and this ... disruption is causing a chain reaction of more disruption and more chaos.

"Eventually, space and time will become so jumbled ... so mixed up ... so ... utterly wrong that nothing will be right and the galaxy, unable to correct itself ... unable to put space and time right again ... will simply destroy itself."

Quizzel let go of Fizz's hand and stared thoughtfully at her.

"Now, do you understand? The galaxy and all the solar systems and all the planets and all the life within it will just disappear into a big ... black hole and there will be nothing left."

"Zilch," Quizzel's left head added.

"Just a speck of dust floating about in space," his right head said.

Fizz just stared at Quizzel as the realisation of what he was telling her sunk in. It seemed to her that she and Dawn had destroyed the galaxy and, with it, millions of planets, billions of species and zillions of lives.

It would be fair to say, at this point, that Fizz just wanted to curl up in a ball and hide under a space rock. But, since her boss was standing directly in front of her waiting for her to say something a little more productive, she decided to ask ...

"So what can I do?"

"You must find Dawn Gray," Quizzel said. "She is the key. The only way to put things right is to go back in time to the night the pair of you DROSSed off the Earth and make sure that, this time, you DROSS off correctly without any problems. Only by undoing what has been done can you set the flow of space and time straight again.

"Find Dawn Gray ... she is the only one."

"The only one what?"

"The only one who can save the galaxy."

20

mantor

Mantor. That was what every being in the galaxy knew him as, though nobody had ever seen him and many believed in him only as a myth or legend.

But still, every being in the galaxy was afraid of him.

Mantor was a unique life form. There were no others of his kind. He had no species, no race, no kin, no origin; he had simply *existed*, as far as anyone knew, for as long as the galaxy itself had existed.

Over the aeons which had passed since the dawn of the known galaxy and since the beginning of space and time itself, the legend of Mantor had manifested itself over and over again.

Some said that he was as tall as a hundred humans, dressed all in black battle armour. Others said that he was, himself, humanoid in appearance and carried a personal armoury of state of the art weapons and torture devices.

Some believed that Mantor was a Space-Time Vortex Manipulator (a being who could cut holes in time and space and erase moments of time, even whole historic events, even entire civilisations), but nobody had ever come across a real Space-Time Vortex Manipulator, so that theory was hard to prove.

Others believed that Mantor was an evil bounty hunter who hunted individuals down across the galaxy for nothing more than money, favours and rewards.

In fact, of course, nobody in the entire galaxy knew exactly what Mantor was or where he came from or what he did because, in reality, he was nothing more than a myth, a modern, galactic bogeyman, a figment, many believed, of pure imagination.

Yes, the truth was that nobody knew anything about Mantor because nobody had ever seen him.

But all that … was about to change.

21

the visitor
to dragornus six

The velvety-looking black ship hung above the modest little town which sat at the centre of Dragornus Six.

Dragornus Six was a humble world, not much more than forests and swampland really, but its inhabitants were happy and contented people.

Dragonians, as the people of Dragornus Six are more commonly known, are a form of organic life form. They grow from pods planted every summer by their elders. These pods or seedlings sprout and bloom and eventually, from within the jelly-like pod, hatches a new Dragonian.

Dragonians are small. Not much more than two feet tall, they are humanoid in appearance, apart from their enormous, saucer-like eyes which help them to see at night, which is when they hunt for their food.

However, despite their contentment and general happiness, the Dragonian people had been, for most of their existence, regarded as a sub-civilised species. This is mainly due to the fact that they lived in trees and ate wild animals and, for the most part, had not really evolved much since the dawn of their species some two thousand years before.

But, in recent years, things had changed.

Ever since the mysterious Giants descended on Dragornus Six from the vastness of space, everything had changed.

These Giants had introduced themselves as Mister Gray and Misses Gray and they had looked quite odd in shiny, colourful headgear, dark shields across their eyes and covered in green slime.

At first, when they arrived, the Grays had seemed horrified and quite distressed but, once the tiny people of Dragornus Six had thrown themselves at their feet and pledged eternal loyalty to their new king and queen who had been sent to them from the heavens, then both of them seemed to become a little more comfortable.

After time, King Mistagray and Queen Missesgray, as the people of Dragornus Six had come to call them, came to realise that they had much to teach the simple, ignorant little people who worshipped them.

The new King and Queen taught the Dragonians how to speak … how to cook … how to use wood from the trees in the forest to build simple little homes. They also taught them how to knit rather fetching woolly jumpers and little bobble hats.

And, after more time, the entire population of the planet had teamed together, under the rule of the Grays, to build a modest but still thoroughly impressive village, with little houses made from wood and mud and dry grass, painted with various different coloured plant dyes.

And, as more and more time passed and year after year slipped by, the Grays came to accept the Dragonians as their own. Together, the people of Dragornus Six and their new, heaven-sent royalty evolved and learned to grow and love each other.

But now, the Grays feared, their home and everything they had built and worked for was under threat, for a new arrival from the heavens was descending upon Dragornus Six, an event not seen since the planet had first ever come to be.

King Mistagray and Queen Missesgray, dressed in their best, handmade, ceremonial robes of Kurka hair, (a Kurka is a kind of big Guinea Pig), stood at the heart of Dragornus Six's modest little model village, awestruck as the sleek, black ship, glided down to the surface of their planet in complete and total silence.

"That's one heck of a ship," a voice uttered behind Queen Missesgray.

The queen turned to see Arthur standing behind her.

"When did you get back?" she asked.

"Just this second, your highness," Arthur replied.

"Have you found my daughter?" the queen added.

"Not yet, your highness, but I have located her travelling companion ... Fizz?"

"You found Fizz?" King Mistagray suddenly yelped. "Then Dawn must have been with her?"

"I'm afraid not, your majesty. She claims they were unavoidably separated."

"Separated?" the queen said. "Does she know where Dawn is?"

Arthur shook his head.

"Is Fizz with you?" the king asked.

"Your majesty?" Arthur seemed a little confused.

"You brought her back with you, didn't you?" the king added.

"Um ... no ... I did not, your majesty. My mission is to locate your daughter, no-one else."

The king and queen glared at Arthur, but before they could say any more the sleek black ship landed in the centre of the village and a doorway opened.

There was a universal gasp from the thousand or so tiny inhabitants of Dragornus Six as an ominous-looking figure appeared, silhouetted by the light of the open hatchway, and began to walk down to the planet's surface.

"Did it not occur to you that bringing Fizz here would be helpful in some way to our search for our daughter?" Queen Missesgray whispered to Arthur. "We'll talk about this later. You're going to have to go back and find her and bring her here."

The queen's words were interrupted by the figure's arrival on the muddy, squelchy ground of the planet.

The figure limped and clunked its way clumsily over the village's muddy surface. The crowd of small Dragonians divided as he walked, creating a path for him, their gigantic eyes staring up at him in disbelief.

The figure was unlike anything anyone on Dragornus Six had ever seen before.

It was the height of a man and roughly the shape of a man. It appeared, upon first glance, to be of flesh and blood. It had a skin-like complexion, although the skin itself was a dull and weather-beaten grey colour.

But, as it walked, tiredly, stiffly, dragging its left leg heavily behind it through the mud, it was clear that the figure was not entirely organic. That is to say, it seemed to be at least part ... machine.

On closer inspection, some of the crowd could see that the dull, grey skin of the creature was actually made up of hundreds of very cleverly moulded metal plates which obviously covered a skeletal frame of some kind. Linked together, these moulded metal plates gave the impression of skin, until you saw them close up and noticed the scratches and burns and laser blast markings on each plate.

The creature's body was wrapped in torn and dirty rags which hung from its limbs. Its head was hung low, its face hidden beneath a head-dress made of more of the same dirty, torn rags.

The creature clunked and creaked its way across the ground, its metallic limbs creaking and moaning under the weight of its own body. One thing everyone who was watching this mysterious visitor as it passed among them could tell for certain was that the creature was not exactly in its prime.

The visitor reached the king and queen.

There was silence.

Queen Missesgray nudged the king.

"Say something then, Geoffrey. Greet our visitor."

King Mistagray stuttered and stammered nervously.

"Uh … um … well … hello. Would you like some tea?" He said.

Slowly, the strange creature began to unwrap its head-dress, its enormous, metallic-looking clawed hands carefully and delicately unwrapping each piece of ragged material. The people of Dragornus Six whispered fearfully, yet excitedly, amongst themselves as they waited to see the visitor's face.

"He looks dangerous," Arthur whispered behind the king and queen.

"What did you say?" King Mistagray said, snapping his head round to face Arthur.

"Look at the clawed spikes on the armour of his hands and arms," Arthur replied. "This creature is a warrior of some kind. Just be ready."

The king and queen studied the creature carefully as it continued to unwrap its head-dress. They ran their eyes over the rusty-looking spikes and claws which ran along the creature's armoured hands and arms.

"Be ready," Arthur urged the king and queen.

"Be ready?" Queen Missesgray snapped. "For what? We are a peaceful planet, we have no weapons. If he is dangerous what are we supposed to do? Poke him with a sharp stick?"

"Uh ... dear?" King Mistagray whispered. He was shoving his wife hard in the arm. The queen snapped her head round angrily but then spotted what it was that was concerning the king so much.

The creature was now staring at them. Beneath his head-dress was just a shiny, smooth black head mask and there, built into the front of this black mask was a small, blank screen.

"What on earth is that?" the queen asked. But Arthur said nothing. He just watched the figure and waited.

Suddenly, in clear green lettering, a message appeared on the screen in the centre of the figure's masked face:

I AM MANTOR.

it read.

"I don't believe it," Arthur whispered, his face wide eyed and pale, his jaw hanging open.

"Mantor?" King Mistagray repeated. "Who's Mantor?"

There was no time to answer. The screen in the centre of the black mask went blank, then another message appeared:

I SEEK
THE SPACE-TIME MANIPULATOR.

it read.

"The what?" Queen Missesgray said, looking vaguely in Arthur's direction, as if expecting him to know what Mantor was saying. Funnily enough, in actual fact, Arthur knew exactly what he was talking about.

"I think, your highness … " he said softly, not taking his eyes of Mantor, "… he's talking about your daughter."

"Dawn?" The king and queen said together. "What does he want Dawn for?"

Again there was no time to answer.

A new message appeared on Mantor's screen:

**THERE HAS BEEN
A DISRUPTION
IN THE FLOW
OF SPACE AND TIME.**

it read.

**THE SOURCE
OF THE DISRUPTION
MUST BE LOCATED.**

**AND THE DISRUPTION
CORRECTED.**

This last message caused a sudden swell of panic and fear in the king and queen.

"Corrected?" The queen said. "Why don't I like the sound of that?"

Arthur nodded his head slowly and silently.

"Let's not panic dear," the king said, suddenly calm. "Nobody knows where Dawn is, not even Fizz apparently. We'll just tell this nice gentleman that we don't know where she is. Nobody can correct anything or anyone if they don't know where to look now, can they?"

King Mistagray walked slowly to Mantor, his arms outstretched in a gesture of welcome and friendship.

"Now look here, my friend," the king began chirpily.

"I don't know who you are and really, who you are and where you've come from is absolutely none of my business. Nor, for that matter is what you're looking for, and I have to say that we really can't help you.

"You see, we're a simple race of people here and we really don't have any knowledge of any disruption in the flow of space and time thingy or whatever it is you're talking about. So, you see, you really have had a wasted journey. I am terribly sorry."

Suddenly, Mantor's powerful, metal plated arms lunged out and grabbed king Mistagray by the shoulders and held him firmly. The crowd of tiny Dragonians screamed and ran for cover as Mantor twisted his black masked head to face the king.

Mantor's skull creaked and screeched as it turned and the screen suddenly went blank, then a new message appeared. It read:

SEE. UNDERSTAND. DECIDE.

And then, terrible things began to appear.

It was like watching a nightmare.

Nobody else could see what Mantor was forcing King Mistagray to see, but everyone saw their king recoil in horror and terror and begin to scream. He threw his head back, but Mantor's powerful clawed hands held the king tightly and forced him to watch the small screen.

The king's eyes widened as he watched the nightmarish images unravel themselves before his very eyes but still, nobody else could see them.

After just a few seconds Mantor released his grip and the nightmare images stopped.

The king collapsed to his knees, gasping for breath and shaking uncontrollably. Arthur ran to the king's side and helped him back to his feet as Mantor turned to the queen, the screen in the centre of his black mask blank once again.

An image of Fizz appeared on the screen and Mantor turned to Arthur. Arthur froze, a look of fear and terrified anticipation on his pale face as he supported the king. Beneath the image of Fizz a message ran:

COORDINATES.

Arthur could not speak.

The message ran again:

COORDINATES.

COORDINATES.

COORDINATES.

Slowly, with a voice that was barely more than a squeak, Arthur uttered.

"Six point one seven. By ... three five two point nine."

A new message appeared:

THANK YOU.

HAVE A NICE DAY.

The screen went blank and Mantor left as silently and as ominously as he had arrived, through the crowd of little Dragonians, each of whom was trembling and shaking behind whatever they had found to hide behind, their already huge, saucer eyes now wider than ever in shock and fear.

Back into his ship Mantor creaked and clunked and, as quickly and as silently as it had arrived, the sleek, black ship rose up from the muddy, earthy ground of Dragornus Six and in a blink ... was gone.

"What did you tell him?" King Mistagray uttered, as his wife ran to his side. "Where is he going?"

"He's going to find your daughter, majesty," Arthur replied. Beyond that he knew nothing, but, for Dawn Gray and for Fizz before her, he feared the worst.

22

the galaxy guys

The problem with Yinkas, Dawn soon discovered, was when they belched. Belching was a customary sign of good manners on the Yinkas' home planet. However, having bottoms on their shoulders, the whole concept of a polite burp took on a whole new and thoroughly more unpleasant-smelling form.

Besides this rather ... unsettling character (or maybe species trait), Dawn was happy to discover that Binka the Yinka's good points greatly outweighed the bad.

Binka was quiet and calm, friendly and intelligent, a good listener and he didn't seem to mind Earthlings at all - although he hadn't yet realised that Dawn was from planet Earth.

All in all, the hour or so Dawn spent with Binka the Yinka, before the door to their room was blown apart by some sort of laser blast and a quadruple-headed alien stormed in crying, wailing, shouting and moaning all at the same time, was thoroughly pleasant and enjoyable.

★   ★   ★

The being, now standing in the hole where the door to Dawn and Binkas' room had just been was a rather stunning purple colour. But it wasn't just quadruple-headed, it was quadruple ... bodied. Each head sported a cropped pink hairdo and each body was dressed in a rather fetching, shiny, spangly jumpsuit.

It was like looking at four young men. True they were all purple ... they had no ears ... oh, yes and they only had one eye each, a single long slit across each forehead with an eyeball roaming from side to side within it. But, apart from these small, barely noticeable differences, they all looked perfectly normal.

Each of them faced out in a different direction: one North, one South, one East and one West. There were eight legs, eight arms, four waists, four chests, four heads and four long, narrow eyes, but Dawn could not see just how exactly they were all joined together.

"Excuse me, Miss Dawn," Binka said softly and calmly, his arms still folded in front of him beneath his rather fetching black and sequined robe. The four conjoined men began jostling and shuffling around the room, each trying to turn to Binka so they could speak face to face with him.

Eventually, one of the four bodies managed to hold his ground, holding his joined partners away and spoke to Binka. I say spoke: in fact, much to Dawn's surprise and slight amusement, he actually sang.

"It's not gonna work tonight, Binka!" he chirped in a rather pleasing alto voice. "We've come one show too far!"

Binka bowed his head and sighed through his facial crevasse.

Dawn remained motionless, amazed and confused but desperate to hear the others speak.

"Miss Dawn Gray," Binka said turning to her. "Allow me to introduce you to The Galaxy Guys."

Three of the four heads of The Galaxy Guys belted out in perfect melodious harmony.

"Hey Dawn, it's nice to meet you! How are you to-daaayyy!"

Before Dawn could answer, which she wasn't even sure she could, an awful, dull, out of tune voice rumbled,

"All right?"

Binka seemed to sense Dawn's confusion immediately.

"The Galaxy Guys are of a race called Melodaars," he said. "Melodaars are born, bred and raised to entertain. Singers mostly, their one purpose in life is to leave their home planet and travel the galaxy … entertaining people."

"Really?" Dawn muttered, not entirely sure that her new found friend was not having her on.

"Absolutely," Binka reassured her. "The Galaxy Guys here, though, really are one of a kind, and they remain completely unique across the entire galaxy, even to this very day. You see … " Binka pointed out each of The Galaxy Guys in turn, "… Harmony, Alto, Staccato and Bob, here."

"I'm sorry?" Dawn suddenly interrupted. "*Bob*? Did you say ... *Bob*?"

"Indeed, I did." Binka replied.

Dawn smiled.

"Bob? That name's a little out of place amongst Harmony, Alto and Staccato isn't it?"

"Indeed it is," Binka agreed. "Allow me to explain why.

"You see, the boys' father was adamant that his children were going to grow up to be the greatest entertainers the galaxy had ever seen. In fact, he was so obsessed with this ambition, this ... dream, that he went as far as to enhance his childrens' embryos genetically while they were still in their mother's womb.

"The result was ... The Galaxy Guys. A being perfectly bred and trained to sing and quite frankly, not much more besides. One sings lead, the others have been bred and raised to sing every note in perfect harmony with no training and no practice. And all with the added bonus that, for every show they do, they only need to be paid once, as basically the boys are considered to be just one individual. The best and the cheapest entertainer the galaxy has ever seen. They have made their father quite rich, I can tell you."

Dawn was dumbfounded.

"Unfortunately," one of The Galaxy Guys suddenly spoke up tunefully. "Meteor brain here ..." he was thumbing to his brother, the head to the left of him, the head furthest away from Dawn. "... can't sing a note!"

"Alas, yes," Binka went on. "Unfortunately, there was a flaw in the boys' father's plan. And the flaw was Bob. Bob was the runt of the litter, if you like. The youngest and the smallest of the brothers, his vocal chords never developed properly so he had no ability to sing at all. So ashamed was his father, he refused to give him even a remotely musical sounding name."

"So what does he do?" Dawn asked.

"He mimes a lot." Another of The Galaxy Guys sang, spinning himself round to face Dawn and shuffling his brothers around behind him.

"He looks pretty and he dances. Not a bad dancer I s'pose, but the problem is … he keeps on singing! Binka will you tell him! Tell him to stop singing or we're not going on tonight! Every show we do, the idiot tries to sing a little more and a little more. If he gets any louder, people are going to start to notice and when they do … our whole image, our very reputation will be gone!"

At the back of the four bodies and the four heads, the head furthest away from Dawn and facing in the opposite direction was hung low.

Dawn could see it was Bob and she knew straight away now that Bob had been the owner of the awful, out of tune voice which had greeted her just a moment ago.

As the rest of The Galaxy Guys began shouting and shuffling and scrabbling for Binka's attention again, Dawn watched Bob, his head still hung low, his mouth not moving to speak at all, and she couldn't help but feel an absolutely overwhelming sadness for him. What a life Bob must have lived. A life of ridicule, a life of torment and torture. A man who was bred to do one thing and one thing only in life - sing - and he couldn't sing a note. And, to make matters worse, he was glued at the hip to three brothers who could all sing like angels.

Dawn wanted to say something … she wanted to shout at Bob's brothers for making his life a misery. She wanted to comfort Bob and tell him that there was more to life than singing, more to life than just entertaining others.

It must be horrible for him, Dawn thought.

"Excuse me, Miss Dawn," Binka said politely, inter-rupting Dawn's miserable thoughts. "I hope you will excuse me for a moment. I believe I have some business to attend to with my boys here."

"Are you their manager or something?"

"Yes, "Binka replied. "I am. And I am a manager who now has to find a way to replace a perfectly good door because The Galaxy Guys have destroyed it … again.

"It seems every hotel we stay in there is some fight, some argument, some disagreement that always ends up with the demolition and destruction of hotel property.

"But then … that's rock and roll, I suppose. Please, excuse me."

As Binka was ushering the still squabbling and arguing Galaxy Guys from the hotel room and Dawn was laying back on her bed, donning her OCR once again to feel a little closer to home, Fizz's paradise world was about to become a scene of utter chaos, mayhem and destruction.

23

dawn gray * infinity

A Model TX-99 Light-Craft is the most compact and cost-effective mode of transport in the known galaxy today. Nippy, cheap and big enough to seat three people, the TX-99 is the ultimate in off-world space hopping and, as Fizz settled herself into the driver's seat, she still couldn't quite believe her luck.

"He just … *gave* you a TX-99?" Kevin chirped from the back seat of the little ship. "Just … *gave* it to you?"

"Yep." Fizz replied smartly

"He must be wich." Kevin replied, his pale little blue eyes taking in the shiny, compact space around him.

"Desperate is the word, I think," Fizz replied. "Quizzel needs me to find Dawn quickly and this is the fastest thing in the galaxy to help me do that."

The TX-99 was no bigger than a go-kart, but it was flat - so flat in fact that you virtually had to lie down once the cockpit screen was shut over the top of you. At this stage, however, just as the velvety-looking black ship came into the planet's orbit, its tracking beacon honed in on its primary target, Fizz was still sitting up, the cockpit screen open.

"The question is … " Fizz went on, "… where to begin?"

In front of her was a small, black box, a little like a laptop computer but much smaller. On the box's base was a keypad and, hovering just a few inches above the keypad, was a holographic sphere, spinning slowly and rhythmically.

"What's that?" Kevin chirped like an inquisitive child.

"It's called a Locater-Sphere," Fizz replied, cracking her knuckles as she prepared herself to get to work.

"What does it do?" Kevin went on.

"It locates any being, life-form, organism - even bacteria - anywhere in the galaxy. But not only in this galaxy: this baby can locate every being and their alternative selves in different dimensions, spaces and times.

"I'm gonna type 'Dawn Gray' into the keypad here and the Locater-Sphere will show me exactly how many Dawn Grays there are in existence in every possible space, time and dimension."

"And then what?" Kevin asked.

"Well, hopefully, there won't be that many alternative Dawn Grays in space and time right now. And then … well, then I'll have to go and visit every one of them until I find the right one."

"The wight one?"

"The Dawn I knew, the Dawn that DROSSed off the Earth with me and met you with me. There's no way of telling which Dawn is which with the Locater-Sphere: all it can do is show me where the different ones are. After that, it's down to me."

"So we're hoping for a small number of differwent Dawn Gways to choose from then?"

"Well, the fewer there are, the quicker it'll take me to find her, yeah."

"Fingers cwossed then, eh?"

Fizz turned to look at Kevin and saw that his little metallic mouth was smiling fondly at her.

"Fingers crossed," she said.

Fizz tapped D-A-W-N-G-R-A-Y into the keypad and hit 'enter'.

For a moment or two, the holographic sphere stopped spinning. Then it began spinning backwards and forwards, rotating this way and that, around and around and around.

Suddenly, red lights began lighting up all over the sphere, dozens of them, hundreds of them … thousands of them.

A message flashed up in front of the sphere as it began to spin slowly and rhythmically once again.

It read:

<blockquote>

You searched for: DAWN GRAY

Number of matches in known galaxy, time and dimensions: 13,482.

Would you like another search?

</blockquote>

Fizz just stared at the Locater-Sphere in dumb, gob-smacked silence.

"*Thirteen thousand, four hundred and eighty two matches?*" she whispered to herself. Behind her, Kevin whistled a gasp.

"Whoo-whee! That's alotta searching to do!"

But Fizz did not hear Kevin. Her gaze was fixed on the Locater-Sphere and the message in front of it.

"Thirteen thousand, four hundred and eighty two?" she repeated.

"That's as good as infinity! It might as well be infinity. It's gonna take me infinity to search through thirteen thousand, four hundred and eighty two Dawn Grays! We're doomed ... the galaxy is doomed! How am I ever going to find the right one? The right Dawn Gray? *My* Dawn Gray?"

Just then ... an ominous shadow loomed over Fizz and Kevin as they sat in their new TX-99 Light-Craft and, a split second after that, a laser blast came hurtling down from the sky and began to burn through the very centre of the planet.

24

paradise lost

"Close the cockpit screen!" Kevin screamed, as the planet's surface caught fire all around them. "CLOSE THE COCKPIT SCREEN!"

Fizz's new paradise home planet was being sliced, literally, clean in half. The jet black laser beam, coming from the sleek black craft high above the planet's surface, was burning through trees, plant life, undergrowth and, indeed, the very ground itself like a red hot pin going through an ice-cream.

The planet's surface smouldered, crackled, hissed and smoked as the laser beam headed straight towards Fizz's new TX-99.

"Will you stop bouncing around and set yourself down!" Fizz cried at Kevin. Kevin snapped the shutters down over his little blue eyes, which had now turned a fearful shade of amber, and dropped himself down onto the back seat of the TX-99, blubbering and sobbing like a frightened child.

"Who is it!?" he sobbed in a rather squeaky voice. "Who is it?"

"How should I know!?" Fizz snapped. "It's probably Dawn's fault though. I never had laser blasts fired at me before I met her. I'll kill her when I see her!"

Fizz flicked a switch and the cockpit screen zipped shut over them with a *Fssssssst*.

With another flick of two switches, the TX-99 Light-Craft bobbed up from the planet's surface, span around 180 degrees and angled itself up towards the sky.

"Okay," Fizz said to herself. "Let's start at the beginning shall we? Dawn Gray number one." She tapped a couple of buttons on the keypad of the Locater-Sphere and a new message flashed up:

You have selected - DAWN GRAY - 1 of 13,482

Locater-Sphere co-ordinates: 232/5789 – Planet Quambaar Gemma sector, outer quadrant, Frambaar System.

Launch sequence initiated.

Rockets fired from the back of the TX-99 and, at exactly the same instant, the black laser beam stopped.

"It's stopped!" Kevin cheered bobbing up from the back seat. "Oh how wonderful! Oh these beautiful moments where life is pweserved and my circuits are saved! Oh wonder! Oh joy! Oh ... " Kevin's little eyes turned a deeper shade of amber. "... dear," he finished.

A huge fireball of luminous light bolted from the sleek black craft high above them and began hurtling to the planet's surface.

"I think it's time to go," Fizz said, perfectly calmly.

She flicked a switch labelled "GO" on the TX-99's control panel and, in a split second, everything inside the ship went completely black.

The next thing Fizz and Kevin saw were stars, millions and millions of stars hurtling past them at thousands of times the speed of light.

"Oooh," Kevin cooed excitedly. "It is nippy isn't it?"

As Fizz and Kevin hurtled through space, heading towards their new destination in the Frambaar System, the paradise planet they had called home for such a brief amount of time had split completely in two.

The two halves of the planet fell away from each other. As they slipped apart, each half simply disintegrated, devoid of life, devoid of any life-forms or any kind of living organism. The planet simply ... dissolved.

Above the planet's orbit, aboard his menacing black ship, sat Mantor.

Wrapped in his rags, which still covered his battered, armour plated body and his unique face, he sat motionless.

Beneath the rags wrapped around his head, beneath the smooth, shiny black mask which covered his skull, the black screen where his face should have been was flashing a new message:

MODEL TX-99 LIGHT-CRAFT.

INITIATE TRACKING.

TRACK AND LOCATE. TRACK AND LOCATE. TRACK AND LOCATE.

25

empress garcea of grahl

The Milky Way Ballroom in The Galaxy Inn was truly a sight to behold. There was no need for OCRs here. The entire place was so beautifully decorated that it would have been a crime not to let beings who had travelled from across the galaxy to be there and see it in all its splendour and glory.

The ballroom displayed treasures from around the galaxy.

The walls were solid Nectarian gold.

The floors were solid Lympassian silver.

Every item of furniture was hand-made by different beings from all over the galaxy.

And the ceiling. Well, the ceiling in The Milky Way Ballroom was probably the main reason why people visited The Galaxy Inn.

Made of billions of individually woven strands of silk-glass, the enormous, crystal-clear ceiling domed up into space from the top of The Galaxy Inn. The particular

Nik-Nak seamstress who had hand-sewn the ceiling, piece by piece, was just seventeen years old when she started work on it. She was three hundred and twenty nine when she completed it … and she died, of extreme old age, just a week later. The ceiling she had been asked to build for The Galaxy Inn had been her life's work and it was, now, the perfect window to look through to view the Inversarray Nebula.

At the same time every night, 'Showtime' in The Milky Way Ballroom, the Inversarray Nebula swirled by over the top of The Galaxy Inn, a multicoloured swarm of space dust, cloud and imploded star particles, swirling and whooshing past in a seemingly never ending stream of beauty.

As the Inversarray Nebula swept over the Galaxy Inn hotel, the magnificent silk-glass ceiling would become the focus for guests' attention as they were treated to the illuminating, wondrous light show of the nebula, as well as experiencing the entertainment on the stage of the ballroom.

Tonight was no different.

Except for one thing. Or rather more accurately, except for one person.

As Dawn, somewhat embarrassed by her informal dress, shuffled into the Milky Way Ballroom, escorted by Binka, who had resolved The Galaxy Guys' earlier artistic disagreements, she was greeted by an enormous buzz of excitement and anticipation.

Every person, being, creature and species filling the gigantic ballroom was fidgeting nervously and talking to the being this side or that side of them in a hurried, excited whisper.

Many of the strange-looking beings nodded or smiled or bowed to Binka in some sort of greeting or acknowledgement as he passed them. He was obviously a very well-to-do, well-respected individual and this fact made Dawn feel a whole lot more at ease.

She felt that, as long as she stayed close to Binka, she would be able to just blend in and become part of the crowd, despite her still being dressed in her pink pyjamas and fluffy slippers.

"I feel a bit underdressed," Dawn whispered to Binka as she eyed some of the incredible evening gowns and other outfits worn by the rest of the people in the ballroom.

"Nonsense, Miss Dawn," Binka replied calmly. "There are life forms from every corner of the galaxy present in this room tonight, each as different as the next. Do you really believe that you appear so different to them as, for example, I do?"

Dawn looked at Binka. He had a bottom where his head should be, a bottom with two little eyes and the rough shape of a mouth in its crevasse. She looked around the room at the collection of differently coloured, bizarrely dressed guests. Some were green, some were orange, some had more than two arms and legs, many had no arms or legs at all. Some were furry and hairy, others were pale, pink and completely bald, or completely devoid of any kind of clothing at all.

"I suppose you're right, Dawn said. "I guess I don't look that weird at all."

Suddenly an ear-splitting fanfare blasted out from somewhere, silencing the room. Everyone instantly stopped what they were doing or saying and turned to face the main entrance to the ballroom.

"Welcome!" a voice blared out from nowhere, "Empress Garcea of Grahl!"

At once, guests stepped aside, clearing a path across the floor leading from the main doors into the ballroom and to a table just in front of the stage.

The main doors opened and two strange, muscle- bound lumps stomped into the room. They looked as though they were dressed in black tuxedos, but they walked almost as if they were apes, their arms long, the knuckles curled up beneath them as they pounded them along the floor, skipping their legs along behind. The figures' shoulders rose way up past their necks, and their heads, as far as Dawn could see, were nothing more than a pair of dark glasses peering out from above their white collars.

These bizarre, smartly dressed ape-like creatures took posts standing either side of the main doors of the ballroom.

And then, behind them, Dawn saw her; quite the most exquisite, divine, beautiful-looking lady she had ever seen.

Empress Garcea of Grahl glided into the room in a blinding haze of brilliant white light.

There was a simultaneous gasp from almost every being in the room, including Dawn, who watched, mouth agog, eyes wide, as the towering, snow white figure of the Empress hovered into the ballroom and crossed to her table.

Empress Garcea was dressed in a pure white gown which ran from the veil covering most of her face to below her feet, which seemed to be floating some inches off the floor she was hovering over. Above her veil were half a dozen pairs of eyes, three pairs either side of her tiny, delicate nose. Each pair of eyes blinked their stunning-looking lashes rapidly and constantly, but never deviated from the Empresses' seat at the front of the stage.

Empress Garcea's hair was equally as stunning: a mass of floor-length silver locks which twisted and writhed up and around her body almost as if they had a life of their own.

"She's amazing," Dawn gasped quietly.

"Empress Garcea is the ultimate symbol of peace and unity in the galaxy," Binka replied in a low whisper. "She is, it is said, one of only five members of a secret, intergalactic society, formed to protect the galaxy from harm. Many believe that a great many decisions have been made over the last few thousand centuries which have determined the continuing existence of many planets and solar systems that, others believe, were past their time and ready for relocation."

Relocation?

"Relocation?" Dawn repeated quizzically. "There is a society in the galaxy that decides the future of whole planets?"

Binka looked at Dawn, a little bemused.

"It is just a theory," Binka said defensively. "Not much more than a vague rumour really, maybe nothing more than a myth. It is only what a few believe."

As the Empress crossed the floor, she looked at no-one … she met nobody's eyes. Until, that is, she passed Dawn.

Amazingly, the expressionless, emotionless half a dozen eyes of Empress Garcea flicked to Dawn as she passed her and then, they blinked. Slowly, deliberately, each pair on each side of her face closed and then opened again in acknowledgement to Dawn.

Every head in the room turned to face Dawn.

"Incredible," Binka gasped, as the Empress finally floated down to the ground and, almost regally, sat herself at her table. "Empress Garcea of Grahl never acknowledges anyone unless she has some kind of business with them or desire to speak with them."

"Really?" Dawn said, a little less impressed. She didn't know anything about Empress Garcea of Grahl really but, somehow, she kind of got the feeling that, despite the lady's beauty and elegance, she didn't really like her very much.

26

dawn gray
1 of 13,482

It was unbelievable.

"This is unbelievable!" Fizz screamed at the top of her voice, to no-one in particular.

The native people of the planet Quambaar stared at Fizz with a kind of perplexed, foggy gaze.

Quambaar was a Category Nine planet in a sub-civilisation solar system (basically, this means that Quambaar was a developing planet in a solar system which had not enjoyed the physical, emotional or, for that matter, scientific advances most of the galaxy had).

In short, it was what we would refer to as pre-historic.

The people of Quambaar lived in holes in the ground, they ate sand, dirt and grass for their food and they spoke virtually no coherent or discernible language.

"I am looking for a human!" Fizz shouted, mouthing her words slowly. "A girl … a young girl. About my age, mousey blonde hair, probably looks a little dazed and confused!"

The Quambaar people grunted at each other and shrugged their shoulders. A few of them scratched themselves in various places; others simply sat back down on the harsh, barren, rocky ground and continued eating the grass and mud soup they were currently dining on.

"This is ridiculous," Fizz said to herself.

"Maybe our Dawn Gway isn't here," Kevin said, floating just beside Fizz's head.

"Doesn't look like it, but I need to be sure," Fizz replied. "She might have landed here and is just hiding out, too scared to make contact with these … Neanderthals."

"Maybe they ate her," Kevin said matter of factly, whistling to himself as he bobbed around in the air, taking in the sights of Quambaar which, on such a desolate rock, weren't many.

"Yes, thank you Kevin," Fizz snapped. "Maybe I should just come out and ask them if they've eaten any thirteen year old girls lately, huh?"

"Couldn't hurt," Kevin replied honestly. "They might have some left over in the fwidge. 'Least then we could identify her."

"There'll be no need to ask my people anything," a voice said from somewhere behind Fizz.

Fizz and Kevin span around to see an elderly lady hobbling towards them, supporting herself with a stick.

The lady was pale, wrinkled and tired looking. She must have been over a hundred years old. She was dressed in the same primitive kind of roughly cut material the Quambaars wore, but there was something distinctly familiar about her.

"Can you help us?" Fizz said to the old woman. "You're clearly the one person here who can understand me. I'm looking for a girl called Dawn Gray … "

"I'm Dawn Gray," the old lady replied, silencing Fizz instantly. "But I haven't been referred to as 'a girl' for a long … *long* time. Can I help you?"

Fizz stared at Kevin. Kevin stared at Fizz, his pale, happy little blue eyes vacant.

"*You're* Dawn Gray?" Fizz asked.

"I am," the old lady replied.

"Dawn Gray of … *Earth*?"

"That's right."

"Dawn Gray of Earth … address, twenty-eight Kirkland Street, Holsum, England?"

"It's been a while since I've lived at that address. How do you know all of this? Who are you?"

Fizz suddenly beamed at the old lady: her best, most polite, reassuring smile.

"Doesn't matter. It was nice to meet you, but I really have to be on my way. Come on, Kevin."

Fizz immediately began marching off towards the TX-99. Kevin span along behind her, twirling and twisting around and around; he, at least, was enjoying doing a little bit of travelling and seeing some new sights for a change, even if Fizz wasn't.

"Aren't we going to talk to the nice old lady?" he chirped as Fizz reached the ship.

"No," she replied.

"But I want to talk to the nice old lady," Kevin whined. "She seemed weally fwiendly. Oh can't we go and have a little chat, pleeeeeease. It'd be so nice to meet some new people again. Can we, can we? Pleeeeease!?"

"Kevin," Fizz said softly and coldly. "Shut up and get on the ship, okay? We're leaving … right now."

"But why?" Kevin continued whinging as he floated up and set himself down in the back of the TX-99.

"Because *that* … is not *our* Dawn Gray," Fizz replied. "And considering that you have an I.Q. bigger than a thousand human beings put together and *that* Dawn Gray is about a hundred years older than the Dawn Gray we're looking for I'd have thought you'd have already figured out why we have to be moving on.

"Now … can we go please?"

Kevin had no further argument. Fizz zipped the cockpit screen shut and, in a flash, the TX-99 was gone from Quambaar.

27

arthur's quest

Dragornus Six was not the place it had once been. In only a matter of hours the once happy, civilised little planet had become a deserted and soulless ghost town.

Since Mantor had come and terrified every being on the planet, the Dragonians had locked themselves away in their little mud and wood huts and refused to venture outside. The Dragonians had never believed that a creature such as Mantor could really exist in the galaxy. But now they had seen him. They had seen what he did to their king and they knew, for the first time, that there was evil in the galaxy. Terrible, ruthless evil.

In their own hut, the mood between the king and queen of Dragornus Six was no better. In fact, it was considerably worse.

King Mistagray and Queen Missesgray sat on their tree stump chairs, around their log fire, staring out through the glassless window onto their world, the place they had built, nurtured and grown to love. Both of them felt empty and lost inside.

"What happened to us, Geoff?" Queen Missesgray asked softly. "We've been here so long, we've forgotten about our own daughter? Is that what has really happened?"

"I don't know, Sheila, I really don't know."

"You remember leaving the Earth, don't you?" Queen Missesgray said. "You remember that dreadful night, the horror, the panic … "

"The swimming caps."

The king and queen shared a laugh.

"Oh my goodness yes, the swimming caps! Oh I remember them very well, very well!" The laughter faded as quickly as it had come, and in just a second or two the pair were staring solemnly at each other again.

"So what do you think happened?"

"I think maybe Fizz is the only one who could answer that, love," King Mistagray replied. "Clearly something went wrong. I mean, according to Arthur, Fizz hasn't aged a day, which would suggest that our little Dawn is the same age as she was when we last saw her."

"And yet here we are …" the queen interrupted.

"… ten years older, a whole new life, a whole new world," the king finished for her.

"It's all to do with space and time," a voice said softly and considerately from the back of the room. The king and queen did not even look up. They knew Arthur was sitting there; he had been the whole time.

"The galaxy, the space-time continuum, all of it cannot be understood. Lapses in time, gaps and holes in space, things fall in and out of it all the time. Time is lost, time is gained, time stands still for some … moves on for others … it's all a bit tricky, really."

Queen Missesgray turned and fixed Arthur with a steely gaze.

"Do you remember when you first came to us, Arthur?" she said. "Working for the Galactic Tax Office."

"'Course I do," Arthur replied.

"And you told us all about … well, all about that bizarre and unfortunate mix-up concerning Dawn and why you needed to get in touch with her."

"Why I *still* need to get in touch with her, your Highness. Don't forget, officially, I'm still employed by The Galactic Tax Office and, as an employee of theirs, I still have my duties to carry out. As soon as I find your daughter, I must tell her about … er … " Arthur searched his brain for the right word but couldn't find it. "About the *thing* and find out what she wants to do about it."

"But the Earth is gone." King Mistagray added to the conversation.

"Not gone, your Majesty, relocated. The Earth, in other dimensions is still very much a habitable and indeed, thriving planet and, therefore, Dawn Gray must be informed of the … news."

"We getting off the point here Arthur," the queen interrupted. "When you first came to us, we asked you to help us find our daughter. We turned to you because we were new to … LX3 travel and planet hopping and all that stuff and you seemed to know what you were doing and what you were talking about. You told us that you could find Dawn."

"I did, yes. So far, I have only located her friend. I am truly sorry."

"Never mind that now," the queen disregarded Arthur's' apology. "Tell me … for certain … honestly … do you think you can find our daughter?"

Arthur sucked air in through his teeth and clucked his tongue as he thought. He straightened his tie and brushed down his sharp suit and stared right back at the king and queen of Dragornus Six.

"I think I could … given the right funding and the right equipment." Arthur smiled at his royal hosts, a sly, cunning smile that almost betrayed his thoughts.

"What's in it for me?" he said.

28

dawn gray
785 of 13,482

"I don't think I can do this anymore," Kevin moaned from the back seat of the TX-99. His tone was solemn and his usually happy, bright blue eyes were now grey with depression and an almost overwhelming desire to short circuit himself.

Fizz, as much as she hated Kevin's moaning - in fact more than she hated his usually inane chirpiness - had to agree.

They had jumped space and time dimensions 785 times now and it still wasn't even dinner time.

Now, the Galactic record for space-time jumps is 801 in just under 27¬[3] Grakon hours, which is roughly 24 Earth hours. Fizz was currently well ahead of schedule to beat that record.

She did not, however, feel too good for it.

Space-time jumps can have an extremely undesirable effect on the body.

In the few hours Fizz had been hopping through dimensions and times, she had aged more than two and a half thousand years, grown younger by more than seven hundred years, she had grown three beards, nearly flown through half a dozen exploding nebulas, been sick so many times she couldn't even remember and had more than one dose of what is commonly known throughout the whole space-time hopping community as Galaxy Guts. Which basically ... well, you can figure it out, can't you?

It is enough to say that Fizz was not in the best of moods as she passed over a planet called Nytallia Bax, searching for Dawn Gray 785 of 13,482.

"Suck it up, Kevin." Fizz snapped, ignoring the churning in her stomach and forcing herself to be strong. "If this one isn't our Dawn, we've got, potentially, twelve thousand, six hundred and ninety seven left to visit."

Kevin just groaned.

"Oh I can't bear it! I can't bear it! Why don't you just type into that Locater-Sphere thingy ... an advanced search ... you know? Be a bit more specific like ... Dawn Gway, pink pyjamas. See how many matches it comes up with then?"

"Don't be stupid!" Fizz snapped, steering the TX-99 into orbit around Nytallia Bax. "I can't do that!"

"Why not!?"

"Why not!? Why not!? Because this is a sophisticated ... advanced piece of space-aged technology! That's why not! It's not going to ... I mean ... I can't just ... It doesn't work like that ... I mean ... ... do you think that would work?"

Kevin slowly floated up from the back of the TX-99 and hovered directly in front of Fizz's face ... his grey, tired little eyes meeting hers.

"You mean ... you haven't alweady twied that?" he said softly.

"No," Fizz replied, a little embarrassed. "I haven't. It wouldn't work would it? It couldn't possibly be *that* easy ... could it?"

"Twy it and find out," Kevin replied.

"Although, I must warn you, if it works and finding Dawn Gway ... *the* Dawn Gway ... *our* Dawn Gway does, in fact, turn out to be just that easy and we've wasted all this time flitting about thwough space and time after space and time, making my inner contwol chips spin and churn and making me feel like my circuits are going to explode any second, for absolutely nothing ... I may have to kill you."

Fizz smiled at Kevin, sharing his joke.

But Kevin was not smiling and his eyes were still deathly grey.

It seemed that the friendly little robot who it had once been impossible to offend had had enough of his space adventure and was adopting a whole new character. His travels through space and time seemed to have given him a new found confidence and a new found strength of character, and Fizz wasn't sure she liked it.

"You've changed," Fizz said seriously.

Warily… she tapped the keypad of the Locater-Sphere.

D – A – W – N – G – R – A – Y – P – I – N – K – P – Y – J – A – M – A – S

Fizz hit 'enter' and waited.

It took all of a millionth of a second for the search results to flash up on the screen. The message read:

You searched for: DAWN GRAY PINK PYJAMAS

Number of matches in known galaxy, time and dimensions:

1.

Would you like another search?

Fizz stared at the figure flashing on the screen … '1'.

"One match!?" Kevin bellowed. "JUST ONE!?!?"

"You're going to kill me aren't you?" Fizz said quietly.

Kevin span and rolled and flipped himself all over the tiny space inside the TX-99, as if he was having some kind of breakdown or seizure. Then, all of a sudden, he just stopped and hovered, perfectly calmly, next to Fizz, his eyes pale blue and full of life once again.

"Shall we just go and get her?" he said calmly.

Fizz re-directed their trajectory and steered the TX-99 in the opposite direction, on course for its new co-ordinate setting.

They were heading towards a place called The Galaxy Inn, in the Carpai sector.

What they didn't know was that they were not heading to The Galaxy Inn alone.

The TX-99 was being followed.

29

"show time!"

There had been a buzz of excited whispering for the entire twenty or so minutes since Empress Garcea of Grahl had arrived in The Milky Way Ballroom.

Nobody knew why she was there. Empress Garcea did not just turn up at concerts on the spur of the moment; she was a highly important galactic diplomat, respected and, indeed, worshipped by billions.

It was possible, all be it … a slim possibility, that she was such a big Galaxy Guys fan that she had simply come to enjoy the show. But no-one in the ballroom seriously believed that. If Empress Garcea wanted to see a Galaxy Guys concert, she would pay to have them visit her palace and perform privately for her alone.

It just didn't make any sense.

"Ladies and Life Forms!" a compere announced from the stage. "And, of course, our honoured special guest, Empress Garcea! Iiiiiiiiiiit's … SHOW-TIME!!" Everyone in the room cheered.

"It gives me great pleasure to welcome here tonight to The Galaxy Inn a group of guys who have toured the known galaxy and even a little beyond! They've had over four hundred top ten hits in over three thousand solar systems and they are just about to start their ten thousandth galactic tour, this one being the outer rim of the Necrar System.

Would you all please give a warm, Galaxy Inn welcome to … The Galaxy Guys!"

The room went dark.

The crowd cheered.

Binka remained motionless beside Dawn. He was a picture of calm and coolness.

Dawn kept her eyes flitting between the stage and Empress Garcea.

Empress Garcea.

Dawn thought.

Why don't I like you?

Above the ballroom, the Inversarray Nebula span and crackled in its thousands of different, luminous colours, swirling and tumbling around The Galaxy Inn, the crowd, 'whoo-ing' and 'ahh-ing' as they watched, waiting for the show to begin.

There was a flash of light and a sudden, earth-trembling bombardment of drum and bass beat as the opening tune of The Galaxy Guys' set began and the Guys themselves rocketed up through the floor of the stage then, spinning and tumbling back down, landed at the front of the stage and kicked straight into their first song.

It was all very impressive and the crowd in The Milky Way Ballroom cheered and applauded ecstatically.

Unfortunately, this all happened at about the exact same time that the main doors to The Milky Way Ballroom were slammed open and a rather strange, dishevelled girl stormed in looking decidedly unhappy.

The girl, from her pale eyes and wild white hair to her stripy tights and trademark, I ♥ Aliens t-shirt, was very, *very* familiar to Dawn.

Behind this girl, a robot came spinning through the darkness. The robot was bopping up and down in the air, quite enjoying The Galaxy Guys' music as his little pale blue eyes took in the sights around him.

"Kevin! ... FIZZ!" Dawn said to herself, smiling and finding herself thrilled and full of joy to see her funny little friends again.

But, to Dawn's bemusement, Fizz did not look as happy to see her.

30

the tempertantrumous

"We have to leave," Fizz barked crossly as she crossed the ballroom to where Dawn was standing with Binka. "Now!"

"Nice to see you too, Fizz," Dawn replied, smiling, her arms outstretched, waiting for a hug.

"No time for that, oh great Earth-based pain in the backside," Fizz snapped. "We have to go … come on!"

"Fizz, what are you talking about?" Dawn asked, as Fizz began yanking on her arm, literally trying to drag her out of the room.

"Move now, talk later," Kevin said, as he span along behind them. "Hello, nice to see you again," his little blue eyes sparkled as he looked at Dawn. "But, sewiously, move now … talk later."

"Wait!" Dawn pleaded as Fizz, who Dawn had to admit, was actually freakishly strong, continued to pull and tug at her arm, desperate now to get out of the Milky Way Ballroom.

"Fizz, wait, will you tell me what's going on!? Please!? Why are you being like this? What's that little rugby ball robot doing still with you? What have you been up to. WHAT'S GOING ON!?"

Fizz released Dawn's arm and sighed, desperately.

"What's going on?" she snapped. "What's going on you say? You want the full story, *hmm*?"

"I want to know where we're going in such a hurry and why we have to go right now, yes!" Dawn shouted back. "What's so important, Fizz? I'm enjoying myself."

Fizz rolled her eyes and sighed again, looking around the room at the bizarre collection of individuals, all of whom, with the exception of Empress Garcea, were oblivious to the row between Dawn and Fizz going on in their midst.

"Enjoying yourself, are you!?" Fizz hissed. "Having a nice little time, playing space traveller? Trying to blend in, pretend you're with the 'in-crowd'? Better not tell them you're from Earth, Dawn. If people here knew you were an Earthling, most of them would dissolve you on the spot, you know that?"

Dawn just stared at Fizz in astonishment. She had absolutely no idea why her friend was being like this.

In all the time Dawn had known Fizz … at school … and, of course, post-end of the Earth, she had never known her to so much as raise her voice crossly or wag a finger at anyone. She was rude at times, smug, snotty and a little superior. But then, for a being who has travelled around the galaxy as much as Fizz had, Dawn supposed she had the right to feel a little … smarter than most human beings. But Dawn had never seen this side of Fizz before and she really, *really* didn't like it.

"Why are you being like this, Fizz?" Dawn asked softly. "You were the one who brought me here … into space I mean, into this galaxy, remember? Why did you do that!? I mean, out of all the people that could have been saved when the Earth was towed, why did you pick me? Why save me?

"But you did, didn't you? You threw me into this … this galaxy, this time, this dimension in space, with no warning, no instructions on how to get by. I wasn't prepared, I wasn't ready, I wasn't even *dressed*! And I was absolutely terrified.

"And you … well *you* … to be honest with you, were absolutely no help or support to me whatsoever. And now … now I really feel like I'm beginning to fit in … really feel like I've made some friends and I'm starting to find my feet, you want to drag me away again. And, again, with no explanation, no warning, not so much as a 'Hey Dawn, how are you, sorry I left you in the middle of the galaxy to fend for yourself, I apologise.'

"So, yes … Fizz, I want the whole story, okay? I want to know why we have to leave now and where we're going and why you are so freaked out. I think I deserve that. I think I deserve some explanation as to just why you have turned my whole world upside down and completely and utterly … *ruined my life*!"

On the stage The Galaxy Guys were already halfway through their second number. The crowd were still cheering and applauding wildly but the band members could feel Bob getting bored, and already he had tried his hand at sneaking in a few harmonies. Fortunately for them, no-one had been able to hear his appaulling, off-key attempts.

Back over by the bar on the other side of the ballroom, Fizz was sneering at Dawn.

"Ruined your life," Fizz said. Kevin carried on watching the show with Binka, bobbing up and down as he danced along to the music. "I … ruined your life, is that right?"

"That's pretty much how I see it, yeah," Dawn replied coldly.

"Are you actually aware that, if it hadn't been for me … you and your parents would be floating around in space now? Blown up to about twenty times your normal body size as all the natural gases filtered out of you, waiting, just waiting for the time to come when your entire, pathetic little human body just exploded?

"Or maybe you would have survived the towing process and you would be gasping for air on a dead, lifeless Earth which was lying, uselessly in total darkness at the bum end of space. No sun … no moon … just eternal night and you, your mum and your dad and whatever other survivors there may have been, dying, slowly, agonisingly, starved of air, starved of light and starved of water and food.

"Would you have preferred that?"

Dawn suddenly looked thoroughly ashamed of herself.

"No, of course I wouldn't," she mumbled. "I didn't mean … "

"And were you also aware, little Miss Knowitall," Fizz continued to rant, "that I have just space-hopped seven hundred and eighty five times in what is probably a record space of time, to find you?"

"What?" Dawn was lost now.

"Oh yes! Seven hundred and eighty five times!

"You see, there are, at this moment, thirteen thousand, four hundred and eighty two alternative Dawn Grays existing in space and time, including your very good self. And I … in order to find you, have just had to zip backwards and forwards through space and time … seven hundred and eighty five times to find you! Until, that is, I had the good sense to figure out exactly how to find the right Dawn Gray.

"And you know how I found you?"

Dawn just shook her head, still too bemused to speak.

"Because you are the only Dawn Gray in the entire infinity of space and time … the only Dawn Gray in any dimension anywhere in the galaxy who is wearing pink pyjamas!!"

Fizz was beginning to smoke.

Yes, you read that right.

As Dawn was listening to Fizz rant and rave, completely puzzled by the words that were coming out of her friend's mouth, Fizz was actually starting … to smoke. Only faintly but, nevertheless, Dawn could still see, quite clearly, little curly clouds of pale grey smoke coming out of Fizz's ears and off the top of her wild, curly blonde hair.

Dawn felt a soft touch on her shoulder and turned to see Binka staring at her with cautious eyes.

"Take caution, Miss Dawn," Binka's calm and soothing voice said behind her. "I do not know what you have said to enrage this individual but be warned, she is a *Temper*Tantrumous."

Dawn stared at Binka blankly.

"A what?"

"A *Temper*Tantrumous," Binka repeated.

"She is a being who … as a defence mechanism I believe, has the ability to explode and kill any life form within a small space hop radius should she become … angered enough."

A thought suddenly occurred to Dawn.

She had never seen Fizz in her alien form. Fizz wasn't human, she only disguised herself as human (badly disguised herself as human I might add). Her appearance was not her true appearance. It had never occurred to Dawn before, but she didn't really know what Fizz was, or where she came from, or even what species she was.

Now she knew.

And she wished she didn't.

"I would take measures to calm the creature," Binka added. "Before she kills us all. She looks about ready to explode … literally."

Blimey.

Dawn thought.

Fizz is a walking bomb!

Dawn saw the smoke coming from Fizz's ears thickening and a sudden well of fear rose in her throat.

I'm about to be killed by my best friend.

I'm about to be killed by my best friend in the middle of space.

I'm in the middle of space … with a talking bum next to me … a ridiculously happy … dancing, rugby ball-shaped robot, a bunch of weird, bizarre-looking aliens and my best friend is about to kill me by spontaneously exploding! And I'm still wearing my pyjamas!

Suddenly, the cold, hard realisation of her life as it was at this present time hit Dawn Gray like a cannonball being fired at her chest.

She felt like she was going insane.

Which she probably was.

Or at least, if she wasn't, she certainly felt like she soon would be.

"Okay," Dawn said softly. "Okay, Fizz, you've got me, I understand and … and I'm sorry. Sorry for what I just said, I … I didn't mean it. Just, let me know where we're going and what exactly is going on, okay?"

"Oh, what's the point?" Fizz said, slumping down on a barstool. The smoke coming out of her ears and the top of her head was beginning to thin now, much to Dawn's well-hidden relief.

"You human beings … you're all the flippin' same."

"What does that mean?" Dawn asked, sitting herself down next to Fizz.

"It means your species … your *race* … *human beings* will never change. Never. I don't know what I was thinking trying to save any of you, what any of us were *really* thinking, trying to save Earthlings from the Trygonians. We must have been bonkers."

"Why?" Dawn asked.

"Earth." Fizz said simply. "What a place, huh?

"Do you know, Dawn, that the Earth, *planet Earth*, is the only place in the galaxy, out of all the other planets, stars, solar systems, outer and inner rim sectors, everything, in every space, time and dimension that chooses, it *chooses* … its own species, *freely* chooses, to destroy itself.

"Did you know that?"

Dawn did not know what to say. What Fizz said was, somehow, startlingly simple and yet true at the same time, but Dawn could not think of a single way to answer her.

"Earth is the only planet that, in its time … in one of the most sought after spots in your solar system and, believe me, the Earth's spot is *hugely* sought after … I mean, it's got good light, good heat, regular axis spinning, a superb ecology system, clean air. Really, planets have been on the waiting list for Earth's spot in the solar system for millennia …

"Usually, a planet only gets relocated when it can't evolve any more. Because natural resources dry up or because all of its species become extinct. When that happens the planet is relocated and a new planet is moved into its spot.

"But Earth, *the* Earth actually decided its own fate. The people of Earth, through their own systematic destruction of their own environment, their own natural resources, their own ecology, even their own species, left the Galactic Council no choice but to relocate it. Isn't that amazing?"

"So … let me get this straight," Dawn said. "Earth was relocated by the Galactic Council of Trygonia?"

"Trygonia is the official council, yeah," Fizz said. "But everyone knows there is another council, a secret council who really decides the fate of every planet and species in the galaxy.

"They have to remain secret, don't they? I mean, they'd have millions of different species after their blood if they made themselves known. Who knows how many planets they've relocated, how many species they have extermi-nated? But really, in Earth's case, I think their decision was justified, don't you?"

"So, another planet is where the Earth used to be?" Dawn asked.

"Not yet," Fizz replied. "Will be soon. The Earth had its chance. It had the sun, the moon, the plant life, the animal life, but all its primary species could do … "

"Primary species?"

"Human beings. And don't get me wrong, primary does not mean most intelligent. Humans are not the most intelligent species on Earth, nowhere near … Blimey, even most insect life is smarter than humans. Primary just means that there were more human beings on Earth than any other species.

"But all the Earth's primary species could do was destroy and kill, then destroy some more … then kill some more.

"You lot … blimey, you destroyed your ozone layer, you've wiped out thousands of species of other Earth creatures, left them extinct. You pollute your air, you fight wars over the most ridiculous things. I mean, millions … *billions* have been killed over the course of your history and over what? Religion? Money? Power? How *insane* is that?"

Again, Dawn had no answer. She suddenly felt sick and ashamed to call herself human.

"Murder, genocide, greed, blackmail, hate, war, pollution, the slaughtering of innocent animals for fun or fur or whatever … all these things only happen on Earth. *Only* on Earth.

"There is no other planet, no other species in the entire infinity of the galaxy, that is anything like the Earth.

"And now you're all probably up in arms because the Galactic Council decided that enough was enough and that human beings and the Earth should not be allowed to waste any more valuable sunlight or clean oxygen just so it could go on destroying itself when there are so many other planets running out of light and air and healthy ecological systems who would put the Earth's place in the solar system to better use.

Dawn was stunned.

She believed every word Fizz told her.

She believed every word Fizz told her because every word Fizz told her ... was true.

"We failed then?" Dawn said to herself. "Human beings ... we failed."

"You certainly did ... " Fizz concurred. "*Big* time. In terms of the Interstellar Bill of Co-existence and Harmonious Law and Rights, Section 211-B/3, Sub-chapter Four, The Existence of Universal Organic Life Forms, paragraph six, the ability to develop and evolve peacefully and harmoniously in a co-habited planetary environment, human beings failed ... big ... *BIG* time."

"So why were you sent to Earth?" Dawn asked suddenly. "To save me?"

"Don't flatter yourself, Dawn!" Fizz said laughing. "Me and about a hundred other Galaxy Guides were sent to Earth as soon as we heard that the Galactic Council had selected it for towing away. We were all told to find and save any number of human beings, up to five, no more, and relocate them on a safe, habitable planet."

"Why?" Dawn mumbled, perhaps more to herself than to Fizz.

"Because of S.F.O.R," Fizz replied.

"Sforr?"

"S.F.O.R." Fizz corrected her. "Species Freedom Of Rights. Every species has the right to exist and evolve naturally, without outside determination of their future. Including mankind, however stupid, violent and aggressive they are.

"Which actually reminds me ... you have to come with me, now. There was a reason I had to save you, Dawn Gray, there was a reason you and about two hundred human beings like you were DROSSed off the Earth just before it was towed away and we have to get out of here, right now."

"Why did I have to be saved!?" Dawn screamed as Fizz jumped to her feet and began dragging her out of the Milky Way Ballroom again.

"Kevin!" Fizz shouted at the little dancing robot behind her. "Shift your metal bum, will ya! We're leaving!"

"Fizz!" Dawn continued to scream. "What have you just remembered!? Why did I have to be DROSSed off the Earth before it was towed!? Why did *I* have to be saved?"

There was no time for Fizz to answer. As she dragged Dawn towards the main doors of the ballroom, the sleek, velvety-looking black ship was careering at incredible speed through the Inversarray Nebula and towards the silk-glass roof of the Milky Way Ballroom.

None of the crowd saw it coming.

The Galaxy Guys did not see it coming.

Binka, Kevin, Fizz or Dawn did not see it coming.

Not even Empress Garcea of Grahl saw the ship coming.

Until ... it was too late.

31

the space-time vortex manipulator

The exploding sound of the high velocity spacecraft hitting hundreds of vast, clear panels of the silk-glass ceiling was deafening.

Every being in the ballroom screamed, running this way and that to avoid the hurtling craft as it descended through the glass ceiling.

Glass and debris flew everywhere, life-forms dived for cover behind the bar, under chairs and tables, round the back of the centre stage, anywhere to protect themselves.

And then ... inexplicably and, I might add, quite magnificently to witness, the black ship just ... stopped.

There was no sound of brakes screeching to a halt. No sound of an engine dying. The sleek, black ship was completely silent as it came to its sudden and abrupt halt. The ship's nose pointed down as it hung vertically just a few centimetres above the floor of the ballroom.

Then ... there was nothing.

After a minute, slowly and cautiously, heads began popping out from beneath the chairs and tables to sneak a peek at the black ship, hanging in the middle of the ballroom.

Some of the crowd even pulled themselves to their feet and staggered towards the ship, eyeing it curiously.

Empress Garcea of Grahl watched from a dark shadow in the corner of the ballroom, her muscle-bound bodyguards motionless either side of her.

Behind the bar, Dawn and Fizz were hiding with Binka and Kevin. Dawn watched the Empress as she studied the ship. Un-panicked and completely unfazed, Empress Garcea seemed to be waiting for something, or perhaps, some*one* to appear; she looked as though she knew who was inside the ship.

"That's the ship that tried to kill me and Kevin," Fizz whispered into Dawn's ear, from where they were hiding behind the bar.

"Tried to kill you!?" Dawn screamed. Fizz slapped her hand over Dawns' mouth to silence her.

"Shut up, you idiot!" Fizz snapped in a hushed voice. "He's probably looking for us right now."

"Who?"

"Mantor."

Binka turned his head to face Fizz.

"Mantor?" he repeated. "Forgive me, *Temper*Tantrumous, but I think you are mistaken. Mantor is nothing but a myth … a legend, a mere … how Earthlings would call it … bogeyman."

"I don't think so, my bum-faced buddy," Fizz said.

Dawn winced at her friend's crudeness and lack of sensitivity, especially since she was fully aware of Binka's own feelings concerning his appearance. However, if he was offended by Fizz's words, Binka did not show it.

"Who's Mantor?" Dawn asked again.

"Mantor is a space-time vortex manipulator," Fizz replied.

"Oh right, something or someone I would have no idea about, then. Perfectly normal by now."

"I didn't know who was following us at first," Fizz said. "But then I remembered all the things I was taught at The Galaxy Guide Academy … about the space-time vortex and its guardian … Mantor."

"So … who is he?" Dawn asked again.

Fizz sighed, sensing that another detailed explanation was necessary.

"Mantor, now I'm gonna be quick, okay? So you'd better … "

"Keep up, I know, I know."

"He's a space-time vortex manipulator. Space and time, within the galaxy, is laid out on a vortex, all right? Like a big grid ... a big chess board, hundreds of pockets within the vortex's main-frame, pockets of space-time and different dimensions, okay?"

Dawn looked blank.

Fizz sighed heavily again.

"Blimey you're thick. Look, imagine, Great Britain, right? Your country, yeah? Britain is divided up into countries and counties, okay? Different little sections called counties make up the British Isles. With me?"

This time, Dawn nodded.

"Right, now, if one of the sections of the space-time vortex is disturbed, broken, dislodged, disrupted, anything, it sends the whole vortex, space and time *itself* all out of whack, right?"

Dawn nodded.

"Mantor ... corrects problems with the space-time vortex.

"Only problem is, as bum-face here illustrated so perfectly for me, nobody believes in Mantor because nobody has ever come across him ... anyone who does have the bad fortune to meet Mantor isn't around long enough to tell anyone about him, because ... "

"Because what?"

"Because Mantor does what Mantor was made to do. Correct problems with the space-time vortex, with space and time itself, which pretty much means eliminating the problem, wiping it out. If the problem doesn't … exist … *never* existed, then it was never around to cause a problem in the first place."

"So, what you're telling me is that, for all his fancy flash titles and job description, this … Mantor bloke … is nothing more than a murderer. Someone who is just hired to wipe people out, people who have caused a disruption with space and time."

"Basically … yep."

"Doesn't sound like a very nice bloke." Dawn said. "So why's he here … who's he after now, do you think?"

Fizz glanced at Kevin. Kevin snapped the shutters over his now frightened amber eyes and span himself away from Dawn.

"He's after you," Fizz said.

Dawn thought, for a split second, that her heart had actually stopped beating in her chest. But then, suddenly, words came out, surprising even herself.

"Me? Why me? Who would have hired Mantor to come and find me?"

"You …" Fizz answered puzzlingly.

"Because something went wrong, *horribly … tragically … terribly wrong* when we DROSSed off the Earth!" Dawn did not appreciate Fizz's dramatic explanation, it really wasn't helping her to feel any better about the situation she was now in.

"Who hired Mantor?" Fizz went on. "Well, to be honest mate ... your guess is probably as good as mine."

Dawn and Fizz were suddenly very aware of a presence above them. A brilliant white light spread over the bar and fell across them, causing them to hold their breaths and freeze where they were.

Slowly, Dawn and Fizz looked up and were relieved to see the shimmering, ghost-like image of Empress Garcea of Grahl standing above them, smiling down at them from behind her veil, her half a dozen pairs of eyes all fluttering kindly.

"Who's that?" Fizz whispered out of the corner of her mouth.

"Empress Garcea of Grahl," Dawn whispered her reply.

"*That's* Empress Garcea?" Fizz said.

At that moment there was the sound of a laser blast, followed by a chorus of screams.

Dawn and Fizz leapt up from behind the bar and peered over at the sleek black ship. The ballroom was full of guests, all standing stock still, frozen with terror as they looked upwards.

Standing on top of ship, for some mystifying reason, were The Galaxy Guys, three of whom were standing as still as the rest of the guests, their eyes wide in shock and horror.

The fourth member of the group ... Bob, was hanging lifelessly from the others, his chin on his chest, his arms lifeless at his side.

32

---

truths, plots, plans & disasters

"What is going on here!?" Binka roared, as he glided around the bar and towards The Galaxy Guys.

"What has happened!?"

Dawn had never seen Binka enraged before, but she had to admit that the death of one of The Galaxy Guys was enough to make even her shed a tear, and she hardly even knew them.

She went to stand and go with Binka, but Fizz pulled her back down behind the bar.

"Will you stay put!" Fizz hissed. "You stick your head up there, you'll be dead in a nano-second."

Above them both, Empress Garcea smiled beneath her veil and nodded her head gently to somebody no-one could see.

"We were just curious," Harmony of The Galaxy Guys blubbed as Binka crossed the ballroom floor towards them.

"We wanted to see if we could see into the ship," Staccato added.

"See who was flying it," Alto went on. "But it was empty."

"And then what!?" Binka said.

"And then ... Bob saw something," Harmony went on, tears streaming down his purple face. "Saw a shape in the darkness, in one of the corners."

"Whoever it was ..." Alto continued, "he raised a weapon. We saw him too late, but Bob was ready, he span us all around and ... and ... "

Alto turned away, burying his face in the crook of his arm as his tears began to come freely.

"And he took the laser blast full on," Staccato finished, his face stony and calm. "Bob saved us. Bob protected us."

Binka peered up at The Galaxy Guys standing atop the black ship. The faces of the three remaining group members were pale now ... emotionless. Alto and Harmony still cried but their cries were silent.

Staccato, however, did not shed a single tear. He simply held his dead brother's hand as Bob himself slumped forward, his greenish, lilac blood oozing out of the gaping wound in his chest, the weight of his lifeless body almost toppling his three brothers forward.

"Who did this!?" Binka bellowed from below. "Boys … who did this to your brother … to Bob!?"

Staccato raised a finger and pointed to a dark corner on the opposite side of the ballroom.

There, in the darkness, a figure stood. Perhaps, the most monstrous, ghastly, figure Binka had ever see.

☆   ☆   ☆

Slowly, the figure edged forward from the darkness, dragging his left leg behind him, scraping it along the floor of the ballroom, his entire body creaking and screeching and clunking as he moved.

The crowd, waking up from their moment of stunned, terrified silence, all dived for cover again, watching as the creature stumbled and staggered his way to the centre of the ballroom.

"Blimey," Fizz hissed to herself as she peeped over the top of the bar. "It really is him."

"He sounds like he needs a good oiling," Kevin quipped.

"How do you know that's Mantor?" Dawn asked. "You've never seen him before, have you?"

"Never," Fizz whispered. "But The Galaxy Guide Academy has plenty of info on this bloke, they've always known he existed, even if the rest of the galaxy didn't believe it."

Mantor came to a halt in the centre of the ballroom. All be it slightly shaky and tilting forward a little, he still stood strong and menacing.

"Identify yourself!" Binka bellowed across at Mantor. "Identify yourself … murderer!"

"Old bum-face has a death wish, doesn't he?" Fizz whispered.

"Will you stop calling him that!" Dawn snapped. "Binka's all right, he's been good to me. Have a little respect will you?"

"Sorry," Fizz replied, genuinely apologetic.

The towering creature at the centre of the ballroom unravelled the rags which were wrapped around his head, revealing the black head mask and computer screen where his face should have been.

There was a simultaneous gasp from around the room.

A message ran on Mantors' screen. It read:

`*#! //? @##& #$%)(!!`

The room remained silent.

Binka stared at the screen in bemusement.

"Excuse me?" he said politely. "Could you repeat that?"

Mantor swayed where he stood, tilting a little further forward. One of his giant, heavy feet stepped forward with a spine-tingling screech, to steady his enormous frame.

A new message ran:

I AM NORMAT.

I AM RATMOR.

I AM ...

I AM ...

... MATRON.

A few discreet giggles hissed out through the silence of the ballroom.

"You're ... Matron?" Binka said puzzled. "Matron? I don't think I'm familiar with ... Matron. Which planet do you originate from?"

"His name is MANTOR!" a rage-filled voice suddenly bellowed.

Now heads rose from their hiding places. Filled with a new found confidence in the fact that the fierce-looking creature in the centre of the room looked decidedly ... broken, everyone in the Milky Way Ballroom felt they didn't have quite as much to fear as they had first thought.

Fizz and Dawn stood up from behind the bar to see that the owner of the angered voice was actually none other than Empress Garcea.

The two headless ape-like bodyguards, who had accompanied Empress Garcea when she had entered the ballroom earlier, bounded across to Mantor and threw their ridiculously long arms around him to steady him as the

Empress herself glided across the room in a blurry haze of white light.

"His name is Mantor," Empress Garcea repeated, more to herself than to the room full of onlookers who were watching in stunned amazement as she held Mantor's masked skull in her white, ghostly hands.

"He is my son."

"Holy cow," Fizz exclaimed. "The plot … thickens."

"Her son?" Dawn said. "Fizz, what the heck is going on here?"

"Don't ask me mate," Fizz replied. "I'm as lost as you are."

"Empress … " Binka said softly, moving effortlessly across to where Empress Garcea and Mantor stood. "I must insist upon an explanation. Whether this creature truly is … *The Mantor*, he is still a murderer. He has killed an innocent young man. Your son or not, Empress, I must ask what the meaning is here?"

Empress Garcea ran her white hands up and down Mantor's metallic, rusty plated arms, caressing him gently as if she were comforting a sick child. She gazed into his blank, black, messageless monitor as though she were searching his eyes for a pain he could not speak of.

"He didn't mean to kill that young man," she said softly. Crystal-like drops of water were appearing from all six pairs of her eyes. The tears simply floated up into the air and popped like bubbles.

"He's not well you see? He is tired … weary, he needs his mother."

"But … " Binka hesitated as he searched for the right words. "Where did he come from? What is his purpose in the galaxy? Nobody has ever known of a *son* of the *great* Empress Garcea of Grahl."

"His purpose?" Empress Garcea turned to Binka, a vicious looking glare now in all six of her once peaceful, serene eyes.

"His *purpose*? Who are you to ask the great Mantor's *purpose*?!"

Empress Garcea rose higher off the floor now, an air of supremacy and power seeming to come from within her floaty, hazy white image as she stared down upon the room.

Everyone, not really knowing exactly why, instinctively dived for cover again.

"His purpose … Yinka-leelak-taknivadaar! is to clean up mistakes made by the Galactic Council! Mistakes made by me! Mistakes caused by … HER!" Empress Garcea span around in mid air and pointed a bony, white finger directly at Dawn.

"Oh poo," Fizz said. "I think it's time to leave again."

"I thoroughly agree," Dawn said.

"You simple little life forms have no idea! No idea what it takes to run an entire galaxy!" The Empress continued ranting.

"No idea what is involved in running and controlling space and time, dimension after dimension! I created Mantor millions of aeons ago, before any of you were born, before many of your species were even created!

"My Mantor is the one who cleans up unforeseen errors of judgement … unforeseen circumstances which arise while the Galactic Council is carrying out its work. Relocating this planet, towing that planet. It never ends!"

Binka was backing away now. Sensing something terrible was about to happen, he shuffled backwards, away from Empress Garcea and Mantor, who was still being held up by the Empress's bodyguards.

Binka was trying to usher the remaining Galaxy Guys away too, trying to instruct them, silently, to take cover, but the group were all still too lost in grief for their dead brother to notice.

"My Mantor has travelled through every dimension, every single crack and gap in the space-time vortex and, in his data banks, he holds the secrets of the infinite galaxy!"

Empress Garcea turned to Mantor.

"He has seen wonders none of you could ever believe. And he has seen horrors … terrible, terrifying horrors that none of you could ever imagine in your worst nightmares!

"There are things in our galaxy, things in dimensions beyond dimensions that are so truly terrifying they will kill you if you looked upon them long enough!

"And that is what he does … that is what Mantor does... when the Galactic Council has cause for it … when the Trygonians and their useless hired labour, the Likk-lax, have towed a planet and left behind a mess in space and time, Mantor travels along to fill the gap, erase the memory of the planet's existence or … in the case of the awful, disgusting Earth, correct the problem of someone ripping a hole in the very fabric of space and time! A hole so big you could fly a Trygonian Council Recovery Vessel through it!"

Empress Garcea opened her arms wide to the room.

"Understand … everyone! The galaxy is collapsing!"

People were beginning to stand again and take notice of what Empress Garcea was saying. The galaxy collapsing sounded serious and everyone wanted to hear about it.

"Soon, our galaxy and every inch of space-time within it will cease to exist and it is *her* fault!" Again, the Empress pointed at Dawn and again, Dawn and Fizz made subtle movements towards the exit.

"We can save our galaxy!" The Empress continued bellowing. "If we can erase the Earthling! Kill the Earthling! Kill the Earthling!

"Mantor … my baby … arise again and help us … show us all the things you have seen … show everyone what can happen to the galaxy if it is allowed to collapse and descend into a bottomless black hole. Help us to destroy the Earthling!"

Everyone was suddenly glaring at Dawn and moving menacingly towards her.

Amazing isn't it? Just how quickly people can turn on you simply on the word of what somebody else says.

Nobody knew for certain that what Empress Garcea was saying was true, they were just happy to go with the flow and, as you are about to see, try and kill Dawn Gray just because of what one person said about her.

Now it does, of course, happen to be true that what Empress Garcea was saying was absolutely correct ... the galaxy was collapsing ... it soon would be no more and it was as a direct result of Dawn making a fatal error of judgement during the DROSSing off from Earth and, furthermore, it was true that nobody had known before that Dawn was an Earthling and, as Fizz always said ...

"Everyone hates human beings."

"What!?" Dawn screamed.

"Everyone hates human beings. I told you, soon as they found out you're a human being ... from Earth and all that, they'd want to kill you. Flipping typical!"

"But why!?" Dawn wailed.

"Because you're a despicable flaming race of people!" Fizz shouted back.

"I know *you're* all right and there are plenty of human beings who are just as all right as you but, in general, you lot are a menace ... a blip on the peaceful, happy little map that is the galaxy. With your mass destruction, pollution and killing virtually anything that moves ...

"Let me tell you, until you start treating your planet a little bit better and having a bit of respect for all the other creatures you share it with and a little more respect for the planet itself, Earth and humankind will always be despised throughout the galaxy!"

"Isn't it a bit late for that?!" Dawn said. "I mean, the Earth's gone, isn't it? What can we do about it now?!"

"It'll get another chance!" Fizz replied. "And when it does … human beings better be a little nicer, I can tell you. Although, I wouldn't bank on it … I *hate* human beings, I really do!"

Just then, as the guests in the ballroom began surrounding Dawn and Fizz, like an angry mob, Mantor suddenly stood bolt upright.

A message ran on his screen:

I AM MANTOR.

it read.

SEE. UNDERSTAND. DECIDE.

The most horrible things began to flash past on his screen and then … things got really weird.

33

the unknown secrets of the galaxy

They were truly terrifying, the images on Mantor's screen.

Projected from the monitor embedded in his black mask, the images filled the ballroom, capturing the attention of everyone.

They were images from the deepest recesses of space … things nobody had ever seen or even dreamt of.

It was all really too horrible to describe.

Some screamed.

Some turned away in horror.

Some simply stared in wide-eyed disbelief and terror as they witnessed the unknown secrets of every dimension of space and time in the galaxy.

"Don't look at it!" Fizz screamed to Dawn, spinning her away from the images, the pair of them crouching down behind the bar again beside Kevin, who was still quivering, his little metallic eyes still zipped shut.

"Why can't we look at it!?" Dawn asked, staring at the ground.

"Oh that screen of his, Mantor has recorded everything he's seen in the millions ... billions of aeons he's been in deep space. Those images would fry your brain if you looked at them too long. Believe me ... he has probably seen things that you never ... *never* want to see!"

"Like what!?"

"What do you mean *like what*!? I told you ... you don't wanna know!"

"Yes I do!" Dawn replied adamantly. "What's so scary about a few pictures!?"

"A few pictures!? A few ... !? Well ... how would you feel if you witnessed the end of space and time? 'Cause it's probably happened in some other dimension.

"How would you feel if you saw whole planets, whole civilisations, whole solar systems being wiped out!? Billions of people burning, screaming ... and worse. Things you never thought it possible to witness. Things worse than the worst you could imagine. How would you feel if you saw the Earth die!?

"Mantor has probably, at some time or another ... seen all those things! You think you'd ever be the same again?! You think you'd ever be able to sleep at night?!"

Dawn said nothing. She just stared at Fizz, the flickering light from the images whirling around them and catching her eye, almost drawing her gaze. But she resisted the urge to look up and see Mantor's secrets.

"Exactly!" Fizz finished, not even needing Dawn to answer. "Now ... let's get out of here! Before we all get killed by this mob of aliens!"

"How do we get out!?"

"I have absolutely no idea!"

The hazy glow of the images from Mantor's screen stopped and the ballroom was dark again.

The screaming stopped too, and suddenly there was an eerie silence around Dawn and Fizz.

"Now would be a good time," Fizz said. "Kevin ... shift yourself, we're going."

Fizz gave Kevin a gentle kick and the little robot span up and flicked his metal eyelids up. His eyes were still amber.

"Go!" Fizz shouted, ushering Dawn and Kevin past her towards the main doors.

But they did not make it that far.

They did not even make it past the end of the bar.

34

the space-time vortex

Everything was gone.

The people, Empress Garcea, The Galaxy Guys, Binka, the bar, the ballroom itself. Everything had just … vanished.

Where they stood, Dawn and Fizz could see only a swirling mass of space in front of them.

It was the most incredible feeling.

Stars floated in front of them, tiny to look at yet, somehow, in some, strange way almost close enough to touch. Planets swirled around them … shooting stars zoomed past them … mists of swirling, hazy space fog twisted and turned and folded itself around them.

But, somehow, although Dawn couldn't tell why, everything looked wrong. The planets and stars in front of her looked, somehow, closer together than they should be and the masses of space mist and fog were black and dis-coloured and seemed to swirl with an almost ominous kind of menace.

But below them, things looked very different.

Dawn and Fizz seemed to be standing on a kind of big, solid net made up entirely of electric blue light. Thousands of squares lay spread out in front of them, as far as they could see, like an enormous chessboard, each little square crackling and sparking.

Far below the net-like platform the rest of space was silent and infinite.

"Oh I do not believe this!" Fizz whispered.

"What is going on, Fizz?" Dawn hissed.

"We're standing on the space-time vortex," she replied.

"This … " Dawn looked around at the electric blue grid they were standing on "… is the space-time vortex?"

"It would certainly appear so. Blimey … today just couldn't get any worse, could it!?"

"So what do we do?" Dawn asked, feeling a little apprehensive now.

"We don't do anything," Fizz replied. "We can't go anywhere. We're standing in the middle of one tiny section of the vortex. Every other square, divided up by the blue lines, is another pocket of space and time: we can't just … jump across into another dimension any more than we can walk through walls."

It really was the most peculiar sensation.

Dawn stood, looking all around her. Space … infinite, beautiful, eternal space. The stars, the planets, the peace and the serenity - and she and Fizz were just … standing, right in the middle of it all.

Each little square of the vortex was about the size of a bathtub and Dawn and Fizz had to stand close to one another, with Kevin floating right beside their heads, to stay within their square.

"Did *I* do this?" Dawn asked.

"Well … not intentionally, no," Fizz replied, trying to sound as comforting and as reassuring as she could. "But this is what happens when the space-time continuum is disrupted, yes. This is what happens when the very fabric of space and time is ripped or torn, yes."

"And I did that when we DROSSed off Earth, did I?"

"Yeah, well, it was Greg Fawcet's fault, if I recall. Look, this is what happens when the vortex tries to correct itself, get it?"

Fizz knew that Dawn most certainly did *not* get it, so she continued her explanation.

"Space and time is laid out in front of us, Dawn," she said. "Our lives, our futures … our destinies. It's all right here, on this vortex, in this galaxy, *our* galaxy.

"Sure, different things happen, people go different ways, take different routes, but those people - different 'me's, different 'you's, they all live out our alternative existences in another pocket of time in the vortex, in another one of these little squares in front of us. It's all really very organised and very structured."

Dawn was just staring dumbly and blankly into space, so Fizz thought she'd better keep talking just to fill the silence for a minute or so.

"Your destiny was pre-planned, same as everyone else's. When you moved Greg Fawcet ... when you pushed him off you and disturbed one of the light columns in the LX-Dome, you broke a section of the vortex and you ended up here.

"But the thing is, Dawn, you shouldn't be here ... see? You changed the future, you disrupted space and time itself and now the space-time vortex is trying to correct itself, trying to figure out where and what the mistake is.

"Only problem is, it's running out of time. If the vortex doesn't right itself and space-time isn't put straight, the vortex will just get so confused, so disrupted, that the galaxy will just ... implode basically."

Dawn began moving her lips slowly. Softly, almost in a whisper, she began to speak.

"I had no idea that one little mistake ... one little thing by one, single thirteen year-old could create such chaos in the entire galaxy."

Fizz smiled at her friend.

"Again, another human trait and another human flaw. Human beings never think, never *seriously* believe that anything they do makes a difference. They never consider the consequences of their actions until it's too late. Well, let me tell you, Dawn Gray, everything we do … makes a difference somewhere and to somebody … *everything*."

Two flashes of light temporarily blinded the girls and left Kevin spinning around and around in mid-air, like a top.

When their eyesight came back to them, they saw two things. One … terrified them, the other confused them.

The first thing they saw was Mantor. Standing just six squares of the vortex in front of them, he was fiddling on his armour-clad arm with some computerised device which looked, strangely, like a Gameboy.

The second thing they saw was a rather smartly dressed man with a silly grin on his face, who Fizz recognised instantly as he appeared, squashed up next to them in their tiny little square of the vortex. It was Arthur, the intergalactic tax man.

"Hello ladies," Arthur said, smiling as he dusted down his immaculate suit.

Neither Fizz nor Dawn paid Arthur any attention at first; they were too busy staring across the vortex at Mantor.

"Can he *see* us?" Dawn whispered to Fizz.

"I don't think so," Fizz replied, watching Mantor as his blank monitor peered all around, seemingly searching for something. Somehow, in some way, Mantor did not seem to be able to see across the vortex in the same way Fizz and Dawn could.

"Actually, he looks a bit lost. He hasn't seen us anyway, that's for sure. If he had … we'd be dead."

Fizz snapped her head around to Arthur suddenly.

"So what's your story, hmm?" Fizz asked accusingly. "How did you get here?"

"More importantly." Dawn asked at the same time. "Who *are* you?"

Arthur produced one of his cards and handed it to Dawn.

"Arthur the intergalactic tax man," he said pointing to his name on the card. "That's me ... that's my name. Nice to meet you at last ... Dawn Gray."

Dawn instantly threw a glance to Fizz.

"Fizz?"

"Don't ask me," Fizz replied. "This one's all yours. It's you he's looking for."

"What do you want?" Dawn asked, a little defensively. She wasn't sure why but the words 'tax man' didn't sound particularly welcoming or friendly.

"Well, if you ask me what I want in an official capacity ... " Arthur began, "... it's regarding your possession of ninety six percent of the Earth's surface. If you ask me what I want in an unofficial capacity, it's regarding your parents, the king and queen of Dragornus Six and the fact that they want you found safe and sound."

Dawn felt a headache coming on again.

Suddenly the vortex fizzed and crackled and then ... disappeared.

In a flash, everyone found themselves on a white beach sitting beneath three blazing suns.

"Explain!" Dawn just screamed.

"It's the vortex!" Fizz shouted back. "Don't worry, its just trying to figure out where it should put us. Don't pay it any attention."

Another flash of light and everyone found themselves standing on the electric blue chessboard again.

"See?" Fizz said. "The vortex is just trying to correct itself, nothing to worry about."

Nobody except Kevin noticed that when the vortex re-appeared beneath them, this time Mantor was standing just three squares away from them all and he seemed to be looking right at them.

"What did you just say?" Dawn asked Arthur, completely unaware that Mantor was so close. "I own ninety six percent of the Earth's surface?"

"Yes." Arthur replied very business-like. "That is absolutely correct. It appears ... " Arthur produced a pen and notepad from inside his jacket pocket, flipped the pad open and began to read from some notes.

"... that, as you and Fizz here DROSSed of the Earth just before the Trygonian Council Recovery Vessel began its towing away of the planet ...

"Incidentally … " Arthur turned to Fizz, a slimy, knowing smile stretched across his thin lips, "your DROSSing off was a highly illegal procedure and one for which you will be caught up with for before long, I'm sure …

"Anyway, you, Dawn Gray, left a half-eaten … now, let me see here … " Arthur consulted his notes more closely. "… chocolate digestive biscuit? Is that right?

"And over the course of the ten thousand years since you DROSSed off the Earth, that biscuit played host to all manner of bacteria and insect life, not to mention thousands of kinds of mould and fungus and has, well … let's just say … it has expanded rapidly and now covers ninety six percent of the Earth."

"Ten thousand years?" was all Dawn could say. "*Ten thousand years?*"

Suddenly, the vortex rocked, sparked and fizzed again, before disappearing once more.

This time everyone found themselves sitting in a dingy, smelly old prison cell, with a rather hideous-looking, tentacled creature growling at them from the other side of the bars.

"A Hyn-Karian Bloater Frog!" Fizz screamed excitedly. "Wow, I never thought I'd ever see one up close!"

"Um … can I just say," Arthur said calmly. "I am trying to conduct a rather important piece of business here and all this … dimension hopping is getting rather distracting. Is there any way we could stop it?"

The Hyn-Karian Bloater Frog, a pink creature with the upper body of a normal frog but an abdomen the size of a hot air balloon, suddenly began screaming and thrashing around violently as it wrestled with the bars, obviously trying to break in and get to the impostors who had just materialised inside its cell.

"Fizz?" Dawn said nervously.

"Hyn-Karian Bloater Frogs rule the Outway section of Quadrant 1. All beings in the Quadrant with humanoid form were all rounded up and enslaved almost a hundred years ago. Now humanoid life-forms serve Bloater Frogs. I suppose he's wondering just where we came from."

Then in a flash of blinding light the vortex was back, crackling and fizzing and, now spitting sparks of electric blue light dangerously into the air.

"Um … hello?" Kevin said in a nervous, trembling whisper.

"Shush, Kevin," Fizz scolded. "Not now."

"No sewiously, I think you'd better look at this." Kevin pleaded.

"Kevin, be quiet!" Fizz snapped. "Dawn needs to talk to Arthur here. It's important by the sound of it and I want to hear what it is."

Gathering herself together, Dawn turned to Arthur.

"How have I been gone ten thousand years?" she asked.

"Oh, in your dimension you haven't, of course not," Arthur replied with a sleazy smile.

"Even in your parents' dimension, you've only been gone from the Earth ten years.

"No, no, my orders come from Earth ten thousand years in the future. A new species lives there now and they're becoming quite fed up with the heaving, drooling mass of mouldy biscuit that's pretty much taking over the entire planet.

"Of course, they can't destroy it: the Galactic Tax Office would never allow that since, in effect, it belongs to you. No, the only way the afore mentioned … biscuit can be removed or destroyed is for failure to pay tax.

"So … can you pay?" Arthur smiled again and Dawn was left wondering just what it was she was supposed to say.

"Pay what?"

"The land tax," Arthur replied very matter of factly. "You owe a great deal of credits for the land your monstrosity is taking up. Either you pay or, I'm afraid, the biscuit will have to be removed."

"Evewyone!" Kevin squealed. "I think we're in twouble here!!!"

"Is he serious?" Dawn asked Fizz. "Land tax on a ten thousand year old biscuit. I thought money didn't exist any more?"

"Oh goodness gracious me!" Arthur exclaimed. "Do you not listen, girl? Do you not understand anything!?

Dimensions! Think … DIMENSIONS! In *this* dimension, money does not exist. But, I have already told you, my clients from Earth come from an alternative dimension ten thousand years in the future. So … !?"

"So what?" Dawn replied, feeling as if her head was really going to explode this time.

"Can you pay, Miss Gray!?"

Dawn wanted to scream at Arthur. She wanted to scream at him for being so stupid as to think that she would want to pay a fortune in land tax on a biscuit she half ate ten thousand years ago and which was now sitting on a planet she no longer lived on.

She wanted to jump up and down and scream.

She want to cry and stamp her feet and bang her fists.

She wanted to slap Fizz and Arthur and even kick Kevin.

But she didn't. What was the point? There wasn't any, of course, there just wasn't.

Instead, Dawn simply shook her head.

"No … " she said. "I do not want to pay. You have my permission to destroy the mutated chocolate biscuit."

"Very well," Arthur replied.

"Now," Dawn said. "What about my mum and dad?"

Suddenly, the whole section of the vortex they were all standing in shook and trembled, throwing them against each other.

Dawn, Fizz and Arthur looked up to see Mantor standing right beside them in the next square of the vortex.

"I've been twying to tell you all!" Kevin screamed. "Mantor's found us!"

Mantor was turning his head around and around, as though he were looking for something. The device on his arm was still held up and one of his clawed, metallic hands was held out, palm out, fingers curled inwards. A smouldering, red glimmer of light, like an illuminated crystal ball, span in his palm, crackling and hissing.

Mantor clenched his fingers and the ball of red light in his palm pulsed, firing a shockwave of laser-fire at the section of the vortex. Again and again, the whole section shook.

"Okay!" Fizz shouted, throwing her arms out to steady herself. "Let's not panic here, okay! He can't see us, we're in a completely different pocket of space and time. He's just taking odd pot-shots, thinking he'll get lucky!"

"Well, how long before he *does* get lucky!?" Dawn screamed, her body beginning to weaken and buckle now. All she wanted to do was lie down and cry.

"He can't," Arthur replied. "He can't get into our section of the vortex."

"Oh no!?" Dawn bellowed. "Well he's managed to get this far hasn't he? A minute ago, he was way over there!"

Dawn pointed to the square of the vortex where Mantor had stood just a moment or two ago. "So how has he got all the way over here!?"

Fizz and Arthur exchanged nervous glances.

Mantor began pushing at the thin air between himself and the others. He seemed to be feeling his way for something, testing the air between them all for a way in to the next square of the vortex, the one Dawn Gray was standing in.

"I think," Arthur said very matter of factly. "We should be leaving. Ladies ... shall we?"

In his hands, Arthur held up an LX-Dome.

"An LX-Dome?" Fizz said, beaming at the device. "How did you get your hands on one of those?"

"It isn't just you Galaxy Guides who get all the flashy gadgets you know," Arthur said defensively. "In my line of work, LX-Domes come as standard tools of the trade. Shall we?"

"Let me have a look at that a second, will you?" Fizz said.

Arthur held the LX-Dome out and Fizz snatched it away from his grasp and instantly began programming the dial at the device's tip.

"Right, Dawn," Fizz said, busily hitting buttons. "Get ready to shoot back through time."

"Now hang on a minute!" Arthur protested. "I have been instructed to take Dawn back to her parents on Dragornus Six!"

"Yeah? And I've been instructed to save the galaxy from complete and total destruction … so I think my needs are greater right now, don't you matey!? Dawn, get ready!"

Fizz pointed to the black bag which was still tied around Dawn's waist and, immediately, Dawn understood.

"Wait!" Arthur screamed. "The King and Queen of Dragornus Six want to see their daughter!"

"Listen … Arthur," Fizz said, as she and Dawn began getting themselves ready. Stretching the swimming hats over their heads … stuffing gum into their mouths, putting on their glasses and earmuffs and covering themselves in sunblock and Vaseline.

"If you don't shut it, the King and Queen of Dragornus Six aren't going to have any daughter to see ever again! Or any planet! Or even any galaxy, you get me?"

From nowhere, Kevin suddenly crashed to the ground and began rolling around the electric blue boundary of the square of the vortex.

Wailing and screaming wildly, his little, silvery metallic body zipped around the square like a bouncy rubber ball, just pinging from side to side.

After just a moment or two, Kevin rolled to a stop on the floor, shuddering and jerking as smoke filtered up from his body.

"Kevin!?" Fizz bellowed as she crouched by his side.

Slowly, Kevin fluttered his shutters open, revealing his pale blue, friendly little eyes.

"Kevin, what happened?" Fizz asked. But Kevin did not answer. Instead, as Fizz looked at him through tearful, confused eyes, Kevin's eyes turned grey and lifeless and he stopped shuddering and jerking.

"KEVIN!" Fizz screamed, tears streaming down her cheeks. "Kevin! Wake up! Kevin!? Wake up and be annoying again! PLEASE! KEVIN!?"

As Fizz tried to lift the little shutters over Kevin's once cheerful blue eyes, trying desperately but hopelessly to wake him, there was another flash of light.

"Fizz!" Dawn screamed, the second her eyes adjusted and could focus again. "Look out!"

But it was too late. Mantor reached down and wrapped his powerful grip around Fizz's throat and yanked her off her feet.

Fizz dropped the LX-Dome as Mantor held her up in front of his screen and the device rolled along the floor of the vortex, way out of anyone's reach.

As she stared at the blank screen embedded in Mantor's skull, Fizz saw a message flash up on his screen:

I AM MANTOR.

it read.

GALAXY DESTRUCTION
T-MINUS SIX MINUTES.

GALAXY DESTRUCTION
MUST BE STOPPED.

"I ... get it!" Fizz managed to mumble through her tightly squeezed throat. Her hatred for Mantor after what he had done to Kevin was burning inside her.

"You're just doing your job ... right. You're just a misunderstood errand boy ... right?"

GALAXY DESTRUCTION
MUST BE STOPPED.

The message ran again.

GALAXY DESTRUCTION
MUST BE STOPPED.

The ball of red light in Mantor's other clawed hand began to swell and glow brilliantly. Slowly, Mantor raised his arm and aimed the palm of his hand at Dawn.

Dawn held her breath, thinking, quite fairly, that she was far too young to be seriously facing death.

GALAXY DESTRUCTION
MUST BE STOPPED.

The message ran over and over again as Mantor held Fizz aloft by her throat ... as Kevin lay motionless on the floor of the vortex ... as Arthur stood, frozen by terror and panic, feeling utterly useless.

Then, funnily enough, the vortex vanished and they all found themselves in some dark … gloomy cargo hold of a ship in another dimension, in another time.

The ship, to Fizz and Dawn however, looked very familiar.

35

the hug of life

The space-time continuum was distorting, over and over. The vortex crackled and hissed, and electric blue light flashed on and off through the dark gloom of the ship's cargo hold.

"We're jumping into other times and dimensions again," Dawn said to herself. "Space and time just can't decide where we should be."

"Well done, genius!" Fizz choked through Mantor's powerful grip. "You're finally getting it, just as we're all about to die. Congratulations!"

Mantor pulled his armour-clad arm back, still aiming the glowing red ball at Dawn. The ball of condensed laser power fizzed and spat viciously, ready to be fired from Mantor's hand and obliterate whatever it hit.

Namely … Dawn.

And then … bizarrely, Mantor's grip was gone from Fizz's throat.

Fizz collapsed to the floor in a heap.

The ball of laser power fired, off and upwards hitting the ceiling, burning and melting an enormous hole in it. Mantor was sent crashing to the ground by something Dawn had absolutely no clue about, but which Fizz recognised instantly as … a giant hug.

"Jowlox, my main man!" Fizz screamed in joy.

"Who?" Arthur said.

"Jowlox?" Dawn said. "*That's* Jowlox the One? How come?"

"It's a long story," Fizz said, grinning at the gigantic, squelching lump of rubbery, drooling flesh and the smacking red lips which covered it.

"Jowlox has detected life forms on his ship again, and this is his way of trying to encourage us to stay."

Dawn just stared at the oozing lump that was crushing Mantor beneath it.

"Oh … okay," she said

"Just call it … the hug of life," Fizz said.

"Fizz … " Dawn said, still staring at Jowlox. "Where are we?"

"Astoundingly … we seem to be back on the Trygonian Recovery Vessel, the one that's about to go and tow the Earth away."

"That's what I thought," Dawn said. "So, then, we're back to where we needed to get back to?"

Fizz didn't answer Dawn. She ran to the exit hatch and pushed a button beside the door. Instantly, the doorway zipped up and Fizz sprinted out into the corridor.

"*Exactly* to where we needed to get back to," Fizz replied. Dawn ran over to where her friend was standing, by a porthole window.

Far below them, they could see the Earth … they could see Holsum … they could see Kirkland Street and, very faintly, the tiny shapes of Dawns' neighbours running around in terrified panic.

"The ship hasn't picked the Earth up yet," Fizz said. "All we need to do is DROSS on down to the Earth's surface."

Dawn looked at Fizz questioningly.

"What are the chances of this happening though, really? I mean, getting back to exactly where we needed to be … *exactly*?" She asked.

"Ooh, I'd say about seven hundred and fifty two billion to one," Fizz replied. "But that's just off the top of my head.

"Now, I have the DROSS co-ordinates programmed into the LX-Dome so … without further ado … if I can just find where I dropped the thing … "

Suddenly, from back inside the cargo hold, a strange series of beeping sounds filled the air. They seemed to be coming from underneath Jowlox the One.

"You hear that?" Arthur said, listening intently.

"Yeah, "Fizz replied, as she and Dawn wandered back through the exit hatch. "What is it?"

"It's coming from under that ... thing," Dawn pointed at Jowlox.

And then they all saw it.

As Jowlox oozed and smacked and drooled, from beneath him the sprawled body of the decrepit, now half-dead Mantor was ... beeping.

The device he had been fiddling with on his arm earlier was now beeping quietly. On Mantor's cracked screen a new message was flashing, this time, in red.

It read:

GALAXY DESTRUCTION MUST BE STOPPED.

SELF-DESTRUCT INITIATED.

SELF DESTRUCT IN 10 SECONDS.

9 ... 8 ... 7 ... 6 ... 5 ...

"Oh poo," Fizz said.

There was a tinkling sound from the floor below them.

Fizz, Dawn and Arthur span round to see Kevin, rolling his battered, useless little metal body around towards them.

In front of him, as he pushed it along like a dog would push a ball with his nose, was the LX-Dome.

Sticking out of the top of it a little piece of material which had something written on it.

OKAY YOU CAN PULL NOW!

it read.

4 . . . 3 . . . 2 . . .

Fizz grabbed a hold of Dawn's arm and the pair threw themselves at the LX-Dome, landing on top of it, the pair of them both grappling to get a hold of the little device.

Mantor's monitor read:

1 . . . 0 . . .

SELF DESTRUCT.

And then …

The LX Dome shot up all around them.

The columns of brilliant white shot out from the ground.

And the last thing Dawn and Fizz saw was Mantor, reaching out to them, desperate and dying.

And then … there was nothing.

36

home

The first thing Dawn noticed was the smell of the grass on her front lawn. It was the most beautiful thing she had ever smelled.

Then she opened her eyes and saw the panic and the fear on everyone's faces, as they went running around looking for somewhere to take cover from the giant, screwdriver-shaped ship that was upending itself high above them in the night sky.

"Good to be home?" Fizz said calmly.

Dawn smiled a little ironically.

"It would be … if I thought I could stay."

"'Fraid not, mate," Fizz replied. "We gotta leave … again. But look at it this way … you have just saved the galaxy."

"Have I?" Dawn said, as people rushed and screamed all around her.

"Mantor still self destructed didn't he? Killed Jowlox, Kevin and Arthur. Bob the Galaxy Guy is dead."

"But the universe is intact," Fizz replied. "At least it will be, as soon as we DROSS off again and make sure we do it without any mistakes this time.

"Which reminds me, we'd better get going. There were only six minutes left before the galaxy destroys itself; can't be much time left now. Come on!"

Fizz and Dawn made their way across the lawn, through the crowds of terrified neighbours, to where Dawn's parents were waiting, dressed as they had been before… utterly ridiculously in their own LX travel-friendly attire and with the thing that looked like a firework still stuck in the middle of the grass, with the tag hanging out which read:

DO NOT PULL!

Dawn smiled when they reached her mum and dad.

"Where have you two been?" her mother screamed. "Your father and I have been sitting here like a couple of prize prunes! Have you seen that thing up there above us? Fizz, will you please explain what's about to happen."

Dawn and Fizz smiled at each other.

"Nothing to worry about Queen … er … I mean Mrs Gray. Nothing to worry about, not this time."

"What are you talking about, not *this* time?" Dawn's mother said. "Geoffrey, do you know what the girl is on about?"

The tag on the firework-looking thingy read:

OKAY YOU CAN PULL NOW!

Suddenly, Fizz jumped up walked across the lawn.

"Where are you going?" Dawn asked. "Don't we have to be going?"

"Forgot something," Fizz replied. "Hang on a sec."

Fizz wandered over to where Greg Fawcet was stomping across the lawn towards the Gray family and, without a moment's hesitation, she kicked him hard on the shin. Greg Fawcet fell to the ground in a heap, clutching his shin in absolute agony.

"All your brains," Dawn said, smiling as Fizz sat herself back down in their little circle. "All the wonders of the galaxy you've seen and all you can do is kick him in the shins? Isn't there some sort of ray-gun you could have used to stun him or something?"

"Ray-gun?" Fizz repeated. "What is it with you and ray-guns? You crack me up, Dawn. What do you think this is, Star Trek?"

And with that, Fizz pulled the tag and the dome zipped up around them and the columns of light began shooting from the ground again.

"Why me!?" Dawn shouted, a lot more comfortable this time around with what was happening to her.

"Huh!?" Fizz shouted back.

"You never answered my question!" Dawn screamed. "The one I asked you back in the ballroom! Why I was selected to be evacuated from Earth! Why me? Why did you choose me!?"

"I can't hear a word you're saying!" Fizz said.

And with that, the last of the columns of light shot from the ground and the dome, with Fizz, Dawn and both her parents sitting in it … was gone.

A second later … gravity stopped and the Earth ceased spinning.

The planet … *our* planet … was beginning its journey to a new home.

No-one left on the planet's surface would survive.

epilogue

Something had gone wrong.

Of course it had.

Had she *really* expected it to go right?

Dawn sat, dressed as she had been in her swimming hat, glasses, and earmuffs, smothered in Vaseline and sunblock, staring out at the dry, desolate, barren wasteland in front of her.

There was nothing for miles. As far as her eyes could see, only rocks and sand and dry, cracked ground.

And then ... they began to appear.

Figures from behind the rocks. One or two at first, then a few more, then a few more.

Soon there were hundreds of them, maybe even thousands. All of them appearing from behind rocks, from every angle around Dawn and from every distance away.

Some were only dots on the horizon, some were very close by. But for all of them, Dawn Gray could be certain of one thing.

All the figures were dressed exactly the same and looked exactly the same.

They had long, mousey hair.

They wore pink pyjamas and fluffy white slippers.

And they all looked like her.

"Another one?" one of the 'Dawn Grays' said.

"They always come here!" another one called out.

"That's Fizz for you … never got it right. Still hasn't got it right by the looks of things; this one's even wearing the swimming hat and earmuffs. Oh well, one more won't make any difference, will it?"

Dawn Gray … *our* Dawn Gray … held her head in disbelief as she sat beneath the planet's two blazing, merciless suns, sunblock running beneath her sunglasses and onto her hands.

"FIZZ!!" She screamed. "What have you done to me NOW!!?? FIZZ!!"

Dawn Gray could have collapsed in tears.

She could have given up on her life, there and then.

She could have resigned herself to the fact that, with the Earth gone and her parents lost again, there was nothing else for her.

But she didn't.

Instead, as she sat in the middle of the barren, desolate wasteland she now found herself in, surrounded by thousands of other 'Dawn Grays', all she could do was smile to herself.

She'd just had the most brilliant idea …